"We need to cut some corners until Daddy finds a job and my Lavender Lady sales pick up," Sharon's mother said.

"What kind of corners?" Sharon asked suspiciously.

"Like your allowance, for one thing," said her father.

"*What?*" Sharon cried, slumping into a chair. This was a disaster!

"We're also cutting out your flute lessons," Mrs. Fuller added.

Sharon perked up a bit. "Really?"

"We figured you wouldn't be too upset about that," her father said.

"Don't you think this is too much for me to take all at once?" Sharon asked. "Maybe a little allowance would make me feel better."

"Nice try," Mr. Fuller muttered.

Sharon sighed loudly. "Being poor is such a nightmare."

"Stop acting so spoiled, Sharon," her mother said firmly. "We're *not* poor. We're just spending less."

"What's the difference?" Sharon said, and flounced out of the room.

Meet all the kids in McCracken's Class:

And coming soon:

McCracken's
CLASS

#6

SHARON PLAYS IT COOL

by Diana Oliver

BULLSEYE BOOKS
Random House New York

To Diana Weyn Gonzalez,
with love

A BULLSEYE BOOK PUBLISHED BY RANDOM HOUSE, INC.

Copyright © 1994 by Random House, Inc.
Cover design by Michaelis/Carpelis Design Associates, Inc.
Cover art copyright © 1994 by Melodye Rosales. All rights reserved
under International and Pan-American Copyright Conventions.
Published in the United States by Random House, Inc., New York,
and simultaneously in Canada
by Random House of Canada Limited, Toronto.
Library of Congress Catalog Card Number: 93-85235
ISBN: 0-679-85476-2
RL: 4.4

Manufactured in the United States of America
10 9 8 7 6 5 4 3 2 1

MCCRACKEN'S CLASS is a trademark of Random House, Inc.

"Oh no!" Sharon Fuller cried as she and her friends were nearly out of the schoolyard. "I don't have my hat. I must have left it in the auditorium during assembly."

"Go back and get it," said Sylvie Levine. "We'll wait for you outside the park."

"But hurry up, Fuller," said Desdemona DuMonde. "We're not hanging here forever."

Sharon ran back across the schoolyard. She tugged at the tall green side door. Luckily, it was still open.

Her cowboy boots clattered down the hallways of Martin Luther King, Jr., Elementary as she headed for the auditorium. When she got there, she pushed open the door. Even though school was out, kids were sitting in the front rows. Sharon knew why they were there. During assembly Ms. Tillman, the principal, had announced that their school, which everyone called MLK, Jr., for short, was going to start its own orchestra. Anyone interested in trying out was supposed to meet after school today and tomorrow.

With her head ducked down, Sharon hurried toward the front of the auditorium. That was where she'd been sitting along with the rest of Ms. McCracken's fifth-grade class.

She quickly spotted her denim baseball cap with the rhinestone-and-fabric-paint designs. It was lying on the floor beneath a seat. Boy, was she glad to see that cap. She'd stayed up late last night putting in the rhinestones herself with her new stud-punching machine. Then she'd dabbed the fabric paint on with a sponge. It was extremely cool.

"Excuse me, excuse me," she said briskly, as she pushed past the kids who were seated.

"Hey, watch it, diphead!" shouted Ronnie Smith, the biggest and toughest girl in Ms. McCracken's class. "You stomped on my toe."

"Sorry," said Sharon. If it had been anyone else, Sharon would have told them to chill out. But no one messed with Ronnie.

Suddenly, the strangeness of the idea that Ronnie was there struck her. As much as she hated talking to the girl, she just had to ask. "Ronnie, *you're* trying out for orchestra?"

Ronnie made a face. "McCracken is making me. It's that or go to Tillman for detention, and she makes you do all that charity stuff."

Ms. Tillman had recently begun a new program in which school rule breakers were assigned to do work around the neighborhood. Kids did things like cleaning up the park, helping in the homeless shelter, and working with handicapped kids in an art program at the library.

"Do you play an instrument?" Sharon asked, still curious. She couldn't imagine Ronnie Smith, who pounded kids into the ground just for fun, playing any instrument.

"Naw. I just told McCracken I played drums."

Sharon nodded as she picked up her cap. It made sense that Ronnie had picked something she could pound on. Still, only Ronnie would have the nerve to lie to Ms. McCracken. Their teacher was the meanest, strictest teacher in the whole school.

Sharon fitted her cap snugly over her wavy dark brown hair and tugged the brim down for the perfect effect. Then she slipped back past Ronnie and the other kids in the aisle. She was about to leave when she spotted pretty, delicate-looking Sasha Sommers

3

sitting with Rosa Santiago. She waved to them.

Sasha motioned for her to come over. "I can only stay a second," Sharon said, slipping into an aisle chair beside them. "I just came back to get my cap."

"Aren't you trying out?" Rosa asked.

"Are you crazy?" said Sharon. "My parents *make* me take flute lessons. What a bore!"

"I think playing in an orchestra will be fun," said Rosa.

You would, thought Sharon. Rosa was sweet, but what a geek! She was the smartest kid in the class. And on a scale of one to ten, her fashion sense was a zero. Lately she'd been hanging out with cool Annie Tuzmarti and she'd been looking a little better. If Annie liked her, and Sasha liked her, then Sharon figured Rosa must be okay. But she was still definitely a geek.

"I'd better get going," said Sharon, suddenly remembering that Annie and Sylvie were waiting for her outside. "See ya."

Just as Sharon was on her way to the door, the handsome young music teacher, Mr. LaSalle, walked in. "Hi, Sharon," he said. "I'm glad to see you're trying out for the orchestra. Ms. McCracken told me you play the flute."

4

"She did?" Sharon asked, stunned. How had her teacher known that?

"I do play the flute, but I'm not trying out," she told Mr. LaSalle.

"Oh? Why not?"

Sharon noticed that Mr. LaSalle didn't look very energetic today. He was pale. And his usually bright eyes had lost their sparkle. He turned and covered his mouth as he coughed. "Sorry," he said. "I'm fighting a cold. Now, how come you're not trying out?"

"I just would rather not," said Sharon. It didn't seem right to tell a music teacher that she *despised* the flute. It was bad enough she had to take flute lessons from spacey old Miss Lavinia. She wasn't going to join a school orchestra, too.

"Well, okay," said Mr. LaSalle. "But if you change your mind, you're always welcome to try out."

"I'll remember that," said Sharon. "'Bye."

Mr. LaSalle continued down the aisle. Sharon hurried out the door and out of the school building as quickly as she could.

Her friends were still waiting just outside William Henry Harrison Park. The huge park—which had large open spaces, woods, baseball fields, picnic benches, and playgrounds—was called Harry Park by everyone

5

in the Parkside section of the city.

"Here she is," someone shouted as Sharon approached. A lot of kids from McCracken's class were there: Annie Tuzmarti, Desdemona DuMonde, Sylvie Levine, Carlos Ortega, Kathleen Stoppelmeyer, Lori Silver, Kareem Jackson, and John Jerome. Until recently they hadn't all been good friends. But suffering through fifth grade with McCracken had brought the kids together.

"Man, that was a close one," Sharon said when she reached the others. "LaSalle almost snagged me into the orchestra."

"So, why don't you join?" asked Annie, flipping her long braid over her shoulder.

"I hate flute," Sharon said. She was getting tired of repeating this. "It's a total bore. But you wouldn't believe who was trying out. Ronnie Smith! She told McCracken she could play drums just to get out of Tillman's community service."

"I'd hate to see those drums when Ronnie gets through with them," laughed Kareem. "And she's crazy. Community service wasn't bad. It was sort of fun." Kareem had picked up trash in the park. The other people doing it, kids and adults from all over the neighborhood, were volunteers.

The group entered Harry Park and

walked along a cement path that bordered the woods. It was a crisp, sunny day in late November.

"It's not fair," sighed Sharon.

"What's not?" asked Carlos.

"I have to spend half of the day in school and the rest of it with Miss Lavinia."

"Oh, that's right. You have your flute lesson today," said Kathleen. "Too bad." She skipped backward, her long blond hair flying around her head.

Sharon wrinkled her nose. "Miss Lavinia's apartment is so dark you feel like you're in a cave. And she's got all this old stuff around. It's creepy."

"It sounds cool to me," said Desdemona. "I love old stuff. Don't you wonder where it's been, and how it got to Miss Lavinia's house?"

"I know how. She went into a store and bought it one hundred years ago," said Sharon matter-of-factly.

"Maybe not," said Desdemona. "Maybe the love of her life gave her a statue just before he died tragically in some long-ago war. It stands on her mantel to this day, a memory of their doomed but eternal love."

"I doubt it," Sharon scoffed. Desdemona wanted to be an actress. She was always *so* dramatic about everything. Sometimes it got on Sharon's nerves.

Ahead of them, Kathleen turned a cartwheel on the grass. She was small, but very athletic. She even had a green belt in karate. Some of the kids studied karate at the YMCA with Kathleen's Aunt Jessie.

"Hey, Kathleen!" John shouted. "Bet you can't get me."

Kathleen jabbed at him with curled fingers. He warded her off with quick blocking motions. Then Sylvie began jabbing at Carlos and Annie went after Kareem. "Is that what they learned at the Y yesterday?" Sharon asked Lori Silver.

Lori nodded. The two girls had been best friends since kindergarten. "Annie said they're studying blocking." Lori sighed. "My parents won't let me take karate lessons until my grades come up."

"My dad said it's unladylike to study karate," Sharon said.

Lori sighed. "Parents can be such a pain."

"Tell me about it," agreed Sharon. She didn't mind too much about the karate, though. It wasn't something she really cared to learn. She just didn't like feeling left out when everyone else was doing it.

Sharon and Lori sat on a wooden picnic

table and watched as the others went through more karate moves. Sharon was careful to find a clean spot that wouldn't dirty her new ruffled denim skirt.

"Hey, Sharon," Kathleen called. "Aren't you going to go to flute?"

"Nah," said Sharon. "It's too nice out."

"Won't you get into trouble?" Lori asked.

"Oh, Miss Lavinia won't call," said Sharon. Ms. Lavinia hadn't told her parents the other times she'd skipped her flute lessons.

Sharon watched her friends for a while. Then she pulled *Today's Girl* magazine from her backpack. She studied the cover model, a tall girl wearing a long dress with little blue flowers on it. The dress had tiny black buttons up the front. Underneath, the model wore blue tights and shiny, blue high-button boots.

"You'd look cute in that," said Lori, looking over Sharon's shoulder.

Sharon nodded. The model looked like a younger version of the actress Shari Belafonte. People always told Sharon that she looked like Shari Belafonte.

Suddenly, Sharon knew she had to have that dress. Before winter break, there was always a dance for the fifth- and sixth-graders at school. The dress would be just perfect to wear to her very first dance.

"I wonder where they sell it," said Sharon. She leafed through the magazine until she found another picture of the dress. A paragraph below the picture gave the name of a shop in the center of the city. It also gave the price.

"Three hundred dollars!" Lori yelped when Sharon pointed it out.

"That's not so much," said Sharon, shrugging. "Really good clothes cost money, but they're worth it." Last month her mother had bought them matching mother-daughter dresses. They were two hundred dollars each. Maybe she could talk her parents into a three-hundred-dollar dress.

The others joined Sharon and Lori at the picnic table. "Cute dress," said Annie, nodding toward the magazine. She plopped down beside Sharon at the picnic table.

"I'm getting it," said Sharon.

"For real?" asked Sylvie.

"Absolutely," said Sharon.

The kids cut through a stand of horse chestnut trees and came out on busy Grant Avenue. They stopped at Luigi's Pizza Parlor for pizza and soda. Sharon treated, as usual. She was often the only one of them with lots of spending money in her pocket.

Sharon left Luigi's with Annie, John, Kathleen, and Kareem. On the way down Grant Avenue, they met Sasha coming home from orchestra tryouts, carrying her violin case. "So how was it?" Sharon asked her.

"Okay, I think," said Sasha. "Keep your fingers crossed for me. Rosa was really excellent, too."

"How was Ronnie?" Kathleen asked.

Sharon giggled. "You should have seen Mr. LaSalle's face when she started smashing those drums. He went completely pale."

"He wasn't feeling too good to begin with," Sharon said. "That probably finished him off completely."

John clutched his head and began weaving around the sidewalk comically. "Oh, my head, my head!" he moaned, pretending to be Mr. LaSalle. "I've been Ronnie-ized. I'll never hear a note clearly again."

That made everyone laugh. "You're an idiot," Annie told John as he collapsed into her.

After two more blocks, John and Annie turned down Chestnut Street together. "See ya Monday," Annie called.

Kareem went down Maple and Kathleen turned down Willow. Sasha headed into her apartment building at the next corner. Sharon continued on down Grant and turned left at Elm Street. It was the nicest street in Parkside. Ducking her head, she rushed past Miss Lavinia's narrow, ivy-covered brownstone house. It would be just her luck to have the old biddy spot her. Finally, she reached wide, store-lined Wilson Boulevard. Her house was five houses in from Wilson.

Taking her key from the zippered pocket of her pack, she opened the heavy, carved oak door. First the top lock, then the bottom.

Sharon's mother was on the hall phone. "Oh, here she is now," Mrs. Fuller said to the person on the other end. "I'm so sorry to have bothered you. Good-bye now."

Her mother turned toward Sharon. Although she looked angry, she was dressed as neatly as always in a beige sweater and brown slacks, a silk scarf casually knotted in front. Her dark brown hair was straight and turned under just below her chin. Her makeup and nails were perfectly done.

"Hi, Mom," Sharon said.

"Don't 'Hi, Mom' me," her mother said. "I've been calling all over the neighborhood looking for you. Miss Lavinia called and said you never came to your flute lesson. Where have you been, young lady?"

Sharon's father took his handkerchief from the breast pocket of his suit and wiped his glasses. Then he put them back on and looked at his daughter. "You skipped flute lessons?"

Sharon hung her head. "I'm sorry, Daddy." This wasn't exactly true, but Sharon knew it was the best approach.

Her parents sat across from her at the kitchen table. Her mother had sent her to her room until her father got home from work. Now it was time to face the music.

Mrs. Fuller leaned forward. "Sharon, I don't like you running wild in the park. If you're supposed to be somewhere, I expect you to be there."

"I wasn't running wild," Sharon objected. "I was with my friends."

"Which friends?" Mrs. Fuller asked.

"Kids from school," Sharon replied.

"That's not the point," said Mr. Fuller. "The point is that music is an enrichment we want you to have."

"Excuse me, Alex, but I think that *is* the point," said Mrs. Fuller to her husband. "We can't have Sharon going off whenever she chooses and—"

"Please, Claudia," Mr. Fuller interrupted. "Sharon should hear this." He leaned forward and spoke directly to Sharon. "I wish I had time to play the clarinet like I used to. Now I'm so busy with work that I never get the chance to play." He sat back in his chair and folded his arms. A fond smile came over his face. "My whole family was musical. We'd all get together on Sunday afternoons and all take our instruments…"

Her father continued talking, but Sharon had stopped listening. She'd heard it all before. Just because her father had loved playing the clarinet a long time ago didn't mean she had to love playing the flute now.

Sharon began daydreaming about the new dress she hoped to get for the dance. This didn't seem like the best time to ask for it. She'd probably have to wait until Sunday night. That was about how long it usually took her parents to forget about something she'd done wrong.

"My grandfather would play the harmonica and I'd play along with him," Mr. Fuller was saying. Sharon knew that this meant his speech was almost done. It always ended with Grandpa and his harmonica. She glanced at her mother. She looked bored, too.

Just then, the phone rang. Mrs. Fuller jumped up to get it. "Let the machine answer," said Mr. Fuller. "This is important."

Mrs. Fuller sat back down just as the caller's voice came on the answering machine in the hall. "Oh, it's just that Lavender Lady saleswoman," Mrs. Fuller said, waving her hand.

"Lavender what?" asked Mr. Fuller.

"Lavender Lady. It's a line of beauty products," Mrs. Fuller explained. "I met a woman in the nail salon today who recruits new salespeople to sell their stuff. I gave her my number just to be polite, but I didn't think she'd actually call me."

"I don't want you selling makeup," said Mr. Fuller. "It's not as though we need the money."

"I have no intention of selling it," said Sharon's mother. She rubbed the tip of one of her perfect red fingernails. "I was just making conversation."

Mr. Fuller turned back to Sharon. "Anyway, Sharon, I don't want to hear any more about you skipping flute lessons. You'll thank me later on in life."

Sharon doubted that.

"Maybe I'll start meeting you after school," said Mrs. Fuller.

"No!" Sharon gasped. "Please, no. No one in the fifth grade still gets met. Please."

"Then you mustn't do anything like this again," said Mr. Fuller.

"I promise."

"All right. But I still think a punishment is in order," said Mrs. Fuller.

Mr. Fuller nodded. "Sharon, go to your room for the rest of the evening."

Sharon wasn't upset by her punishment. Going to her room meant her mother would bring her supper on a tray. It was the only time she was allowed to eat in her room. She could stretch out on her bed and watch TV while she ate.

"All right," she murmured.

She climbed the stairs to her pink bedroom and climbed up on her ruffled pink canopy bed. Reaching down to the floor, she picked up her remote control and snapped on the widescreen color TV.

It was time for her favorite show, a comedy about two sisters who lived with their wisecracking father. Sharon sighed as she plopped back into her fat, pink, ruffled pillow. Those TV sisters had it lucky. Why couldn't *her* father crack jokes and act silly? He was so serious, and he worked all the time.

The show was halfway over when Sharon heard the phone ring again. Maybe it was one of her friends. She got up and tiptoed into the hall. The phone had stopped ringing, but no one called to her. Oh, well.

With a sigh, Sharon went back to her room and watched the end of the TV show. As the credits began to roll, her stomach rumbled. Where was her supper?

Sharon went out to the hall again. There was no sign of her mother with a tray. She didn't smell anything cooking, either. And she hadn't heard the doorbell ring. Nothing had been delivered. What was going on?

When she reached the bottom of the stairs, her mother was sitting on the bottom step, her chin in her hands. "Mom, are we going to eat soon?" Sharon asked.

Her mother hardly seemed to hear her. She sat looking straight ahead.

"Mom?" Sharon asked again. "Mom,

17

what's wrong? Are you okay?"

"They called your father to come into the office tomorrow," Mrs. Fuller said in a low voice.

"So?" Sharon asked.

"They only do that when a person at his firm is about to be laid off or fired."

"No way," said Sharon. "They wouldn't fire Dad!"

"Business hasn't been good at the firm," said Mrs. Fuller. "They let two lawyers go last month."

"Daddy could find another job, couldn't he?"

Mrs. Fuller got up. "Yes, of course he can." That thought seemed to cheer her up. "Now what should we have for supper? I'll microwave you some of the leftover Chinese food from yesterday."

"Okay," Sharon agreed. "Aren't you and Daddy going to eat?"

"I don't think we're very hungry right now," her mother said, heading toward the kitchen.

Sharon was about to go upstairs when something on the floor caught her eye. She knelt down and picked up a glossy, colorful pamphlet that someone had slipped under

18

the front door. "Work at Home and Make a Mint Selling Lavender Lady," the cover said. On the front was a smiling woman wrapped in a long mink coat. She was holding a tote bag crammed with Lavender Lady products. Sharon tossed the pamphlet on the side table and continued up the stairs.

Just as she reached her room, she heard music coming from somewhere above her.

She followed the sounds up the stairs to the third floor. Half of the floor was her father's study, where he kept all his law books. The other half was her mother's study. She didn't really need it for anything, but she kept her bookshelf full of the paperback romances she loved to read. Christmas wrapping and ornaments and half-finished sewing projects were kept in there, too.

Between the two rooms was a narrow staircase that led to the roof. The music seemed to be coming from behind the roof door. "Sharon?" she heard her mother call from the second floor. "Where are you?"

"Up here," Sharon called down. "Somebody's playing music on our roof."

Her mother set down the tray with its bowl of steaming shrimp lo mein and came up the stairs. Together, Sharon and her mother looked up at the roof doorway where the music was coming from. The music was soft and sad.

"Who could it be?" Sharon asked. "Should we call the police?"

Mrs. Fuller shook her head. "It's your father."

"Is he playing the clarinet up there? I've never heard him play before," Sharon asked.

"I've only heard him play once," said her mother. "That was when he didn't pass his bar exam the first time."

"What's the bar exam?"

"It's the test you take to become a lawyer after you finish law school. Your father passed it the second time, of course."

"I guess he must be pretty upset now, huh?" said Sharon.

"He must be," her mother agreed. "We should just leave him alone."

They went down the stairs together. Mrs. Fuller put Sharon's lo mein on the nightstand in her room. "I was so worried about you today," her mother said.

"Sorry, Mom," Sharon replied. She wasn't sorry she'd skipped flute, but she did feel bad about worrying her mother. "Are we still going shopping for summer clothes tomorrow?"

Her mother thought for a moment. "I don't know, Sharon. This might not be a good time to be spending money."

"Are we going to be poor now?" Sharon asked.

"Of course not," said her mother. "We just have to wait and see what happens. Now, eat your dinner while it's still hot. And don't stay up all night watching TV."

"I won't. Good-night, Mom."

"Good-night," said Mrs. Fuller, closing the door.

Sharon ate her lo mein and watched three more TV shows. Then she got into her lacy pink nightgown and turned off the light, yawning.

For a long time, Sharon lay in the dark, unable to sleep. She was worried about the future. What if they had no money? And all the while, the soft sounds of a sad clarinet drifted down from the roof above.

"Earth to Ms. Fuller. Come in, please!"

"Huh?" Sharon looked up sharply. It was Monday morning and she was in school, but she hadn't been paying attention to Ms. McCracken. She'd been doodling on her notebook and thinking about the blue flowered dress from *Today's Girl* magazine—the dress she might never get now that her father had been laid off from his job.

"Ms. Fuller?"

Sharon leaped to her feet. Their teacher expected them to stand when speaking to her.

"Ms. Fuller, I asked you a question. Can you tell us what might happen if you cut a leg off a starfish?" Ms. McCracken's steely blue eyes bored into Sharon.

"You'd have a starfish with only four legs?" Sharon guessed.

Ms. McCracken glared at her. "Is that

22

what you wrote on your homework sheet?"

"Well, sort of," said Sharon.

"What exactly does *sort of* mean?" Ms. McCracken asked.

"Well, I *would* have written that on my homework, but I didn't quite get a chance to do my homework."

She gulped hard. Telling Ms. McCracken you hadn't done your homework was like telling the police chief you'd just robbed the First National Bank.

Two red spots formed on Ms. McCracken's pale cheeks. Even her stiff, bright orange hair seemed to get brighter. "Did you read the chapter?" the teacher demanded.

"Sort of," Sharon lied.

Just then she noticed Annie Tuzmarti motioning to her frantically. She was turned around in her chair, opening and closing her fingers like scissors. Then she stopped snipping and held up two fingers. Sharon knew Annie was trying to tell her the right answer. She just couldn't figure out what she was trying to say.

"Is something wrong with your hand, Ms. Tuzmarti?" Ms. McCracken snapped, whirling around.

Annie jumped to her feet. "Uh, no. I was just moving my fingers. You know, stretching them to get the blood moving."

Ms. McCracken arched one eyebrow. "I see. Would you care to answer the question for the class?"

"If you cut a leg off a starfish, you'd have one really angry starfish."

The class laughed. Annie was always saying funny things like that. Ms. McCracken frowned. "Ms. Tuzmarti!"

Annie's face became pink, and she picked up her homework paper. "If a starfish's leg is injured it will grow a new body. This is called regeneration."

Now Sharon understood what Annie had been trying to tell her. If you cut a leg off a starfish, you'd end up with two *starfish*.

"Thank you very much, Ms. Tuzmarti," said Ms. McCracken. "If you'd read the chapter, Ms. Fuller, you'd have known the answer."

"Yes, Ms. McCracken," said Sharon. "But you see, it wasn't really my fault. There was a lot happening at my house this weekend."

"Something more important than your homework?" the teacher asked. Nothing was more important to Ms. McCracken than homework.

"My father got a huge promotion at work," Sharon said. She wasn't about to tell the entire class that her father had just lost his job. "There was a party going on all weekend long. Everyone was celebrating. My house was so noisy I just couldn't find a place to read."

"Well, I hope now that the hoopla has died down, you will find the time to study," said Ms. McCracken. "Sit down."

Sharon told herself that the story she'd told Ms. McCracken wasn't a total lie.

All weekend long, she'd been too upset to think about school. After her father came home from the office on Saturday, he went straight up to the roof and began playing the clarinet again. Her mother had gone up to her study. How could a person be expected to care about starfish when her whole life was falling apart?

At lunchtime, Sharon sat with her friends. "So, did you get that dress this weekend?" Lori asked.

Sharon thought fast. "They didn't have it in my size so they had to order it," she said. "It'll be coming in a week or so."

Annie whistled. "Wow! A three-hundred-dollar dress. By the way, I'm sorry about what happened in class today. I was trying to tell you the answer." She made the scissors motion again.

Sharon was relieved when the conversation turned to the winter dance. Usually, she would have been interested, but today she had other things to worry about. Like what she was going to tell everyone about her father getting fired.

Sharon shuddered. She didn't want to lie to anyone. But she couldn't let the other kids know her father had lost his job. They'd think he was stupid, or dishonest, or lazy. They'd think her family was poor. It would be too embarrassing.

That afternoon, Sharon walked through the park with her friends. She was supposed to make up the flute lesson she'd missed with Miss Lavinia. This time, she knew she had to go. If she didn't, her mother might start meeting her after school.

"Anyone for pizza?" asked Desdemona.

"I have flute," Sharon said glumly.

Everyone else decided they didn't have enough money. One by one, they waved good-bye to Sharon as they turned down their separate streets. Sharon continued on to Elm and Lavinia Harrison's house.

The house was narrow and very old-fashioned. The window box was overgrown with spider plants. Every time Sharon turned into Miss Lavinia's brick front courtyard, she felt like she was going through a time warp. Miss Lavinia lived in another time zone—a very long-ago time zone.

Sharon rang the bell and waited. Miss Lavinia was so old that she often took a long time to get to the door. This time, though, she didn't come at all. Sharon rang again.

As she stood on the crumbling top step, she saw that the door was open just a crack. Something was very wrong. Nobody in Parkside kept their doors unlocked. Parkside was a pretty safe neighborhood, but no place in the city was *that* safe.

Sharon pushed the door. It swung open. "Miss Lavinia?" she called.

Should I go in? Sharon wondered. *Or should I call the police?*

Then she saw Miss Lavinia lying on her blue velvet couch. One of her hands hung listlessly to the floor. Sharon's hand flew to her mouth in horror. Was Miss Lavinia *dead?*

Slowly, Sharon entered the dimly lit house. The windows were heavily draped, letting in very little light.

Sharon gazed down at Miss Lavinia. She was dressed, as usual, in one of her soft, flowing pants outfits. Her blue-veined eyelids were shut and her delicate, wrinkled features looked peaceful.

Too peaceful.

Sharon poked Miss Lavinia's bony shoulder. She didn't awaken.

Her heart pounding, Sharon rushed to the phone and began dialing 911.

Miss Lavinia sat up.

Sharon screamed.

Miss Lavinia's hands flew to her heart. "What's the matter, child?"

"You!" Sharon gasped. "I thought you were dead!"

"Not yet," Miss Lavinia said with a small smile. "I must have dozed off. How did you get in?"

"You left the door open."

Miss Lavinia frowned as she tidied her wispy white hair into its bun. "Oh, dear. I'm becoming so forgetful."

"Do you feel okay?" Sharon asked.

"Quite all right," said Miss Lavinia. Her gray-blue eyes took on a distant look. "That wouldn't be a bad way to die, though—just falling asleep on the couch like that."

"Don't talk about dying," said Sharon, shuddering.

"Why not?" asked Miss Lavinia. "I'm not going to live forever. At my age, dying is the next big event. Do you know what the poet

Emily Dickinson said about dying?"

"No."

Miss Lavinia lifted her chin and folded her hands. "'Dying is a wild night and a new road.' Isn't that lovely?"

"Please, could we talk about something else?" Sharon said. Chills were running up her spine.

Miss Lavinia stood up. "I'm not afraid of death. I've had a long and full life. As a musician I've traveled all over the world and played for many different kinds of people. No matter what language people speak, music is understood by everyone. Listen to this."

Miss Lavinia took her flute from its case on a cherrywood table and played a haunting tune. The high and low notes tumbled quickly over one another. It wasn't like any music Sharon had ever heard.

"I learned this piece when I was out West on an exchange program with the city orchestra. It's by the Navajo flautist R. Carlos Nakai."

Sharon nodded, and Miss Lavinia began to play again. As Miss Lavinia played, Sharon's eyes traveled along the fireplace mantel. On it was a brownish, faded photo of Miss Lavinia as a young girl. She was dressed in a white sailor-style dress. Her hair was in ringlets. She proudly held up her flute.

Next to the picture of young Miss Lavinia, Sharon gazed at a small bronze statue of a woman in a flowing tunic.

Sharon had never paid much attention to it before. The statue looked a little like the giant statue named Triumphant Victory that stood at the traffic circle on Plaza Street by the library. Sharon remembered what Desdemona had said—about some man giving Miss Lavinia a statue as a token of his love. Maybe it was true.

Finally, Miss Lavinia stopped playing. "Someday I'll teach you that song, Sharon. But right now, I'm afraid, it's a bit too difficult for you."

"It was beautiful," Sharon said honestly.

"Thank you," her teacher said. A faraway look came into her eyes. "You know, I'll never forget hearing R. Carlos Nakai play. And he had such a magnificent cedar flute. How I wish I could own a real cedar flute. But they are so very rare..."

Miss Lavinia certainly was lively today, Sharon thought. Her catnap must have charged her up.

Miss Lavinia leaned toward Sharon. "I

believe you have the gift for music, my dear. And it is a gift, for it will bring you the kind of life other people only dream of."

"I'm not going to be a musician," Sharon told her.

"You have no choice, my dear. You are already a musician. An untrained one, but you have raw talent. I knew it the moment I first heard you play."

She's finally flipped, thought Sharon. Miss Lavinia always talked dramatically, but not like this. Maybe she was getting so old that her mind was slipping.

As if she'd read Sharon's thoughts, Miss Lavinia added, "I'm telling you this now in case I am not here to tell it to you later. Music is your destiny, my dear."

After her flute lesson, Sharon went straight home. She stopped short when she reached her front hallway. The sound of raised voices was coming from the kitchen.

"You are so thickheaded!" Mrs. Fuller said hotly.

"You're living in a dream world!" Mr. Fuller shouted back.

Sharon knew other kids' parents fought sometimes. But she had never heard her own parents shout at one another. Never.

Creeping closer, Sharon stopped outside the kitchen doorway and listened.

"Don't talk down to me, Alex," Sharon's mother said. "You've never had any respect for my brains. You don't think I can do anything, do you?"

"Claudia, selling Pink Lady cosmetics is

not going to support this family!" Mr. Fuller said.

"Lavender Lady."

"What?"

"You haven't been listening to me! You don't even know the name of the company!" With that, Mrs. Fuller stormed out of the kitchen. She didn't see Sharon standing there as she stomped up the stairs.

"Claudia!" Mr. Fuller shouted after his wife as he came out of the kitchen.

Sharon's mother didn't answer. She continued on up the stairs. Suddenly, Mr. Fuller noticed Sharon. "Hello, honey," he said with a pained smile.

"Hi, Daddy," said Sharon.

"Your mother's just upset because she wants to help me out right now, but I don't think she really can."

"I guess a Lavender Lady salesperson doesn't make as much as a lawyer does," said Sharon.

"Probably not," said Mr. Fuller. "And your mother has never sold anything in her life. I simply said she might as well not bother trying it since it won't bring in enough money to make a difference. But she means well, and I didn't want to make her feel bad. I suppose I could have said it in a nicer way."

"I guess so," Sharon said. The knot in her stomach was slowly unknotting. Talking to her father made things seem less scary. "What's for supper?" she asked.

Mr. Fuller shrugged. "We could call that new Mexican restaurant and order." He stopped. "On the other hand, maybe that isn't such a good idea."

"Mexican food sounds good," said Sharon. She loved chicken enchiladas.

Mr. Fuller went back into the kitchen and opened the refrigerator. "No, we'd better start eating at home. Ordering in costs a lot. Things are going to be a little tight for a while."

"Dad, are we poor now?" Sharon blurted out.

"No, no, sweetheart," her father said. "We have a little savings, and my firm gave me some money when they let me go. We just have to make that money last until I find a new position."

"Oh. Will you collect unenjoyment?"

"Unem*ploy*ment," Mr. Fuller corrected.

"Michael Leontes, a boy in my class, called it unenjoyment," Sharon explained. "He says his father collects unenjoyment and it is no fun."

"Unenjoyment is a good name for it," said Mr. Fuller, chuckling. He pulled a frozen chicken from the freezer. "But the real name is unemployment. Everyone pays money into a government fund called an unemployment insurance fund. That money helps people if they run out of money because they've lost their job. Unemployment means not working, so the money is there for you when you're not working."

"Oh. So you mean, you're just getting your own money back?" Sharon asked.

"In a way. Most people have paid a lot into unemployment, so they are getting back what they've paid in."

"That doesn't sound so bad."

Mr. Fuller frowned. "Well, most people would rather have jobs. Unemployment doesn't give you a lot of money. And it runs out after a while."

Sharon noticed that her father was staring at the frozen chicken in his hands. "Mom puts that in the microwave to unfreeze it," she told him.

He opened the microwave door.

"She usually takes the wrapper off first," Sharon added. "And she rinses it, too."

"Oh," Mr. Fuller said. He seemed a little embarrassed.

That night, they sat down to a dinner of tough chicken, undercooked potatoes, and mushy green beans. Sharon's mother barely looked at Sharon's father. When she did look at him, it was with icy anger.

Sharon tried to break the awful silence. "You know, I think Miss Lavinia might be going crazy," she said as she stabbed at her chicken.

"Sharon!" Mrs. Fuller scolded.

"No, really. I mean it. Today she left the door open, and I found her conked out on her couch. Then she woke up and started saying all this nutty stuff about dying and destiny."

"Miss Lavinia is just getting old," Mr. Fuller said, trying to mash his hard potato. "She shouldn't have left the door unlocked, though."

"What did she say about dying?" asked Mrs. Fuller.

"Just that she would die someday," said Sharon.

"That doesn't sound nutty," Mr. Fuller commented.

"Well, I wish she wouldn't talk about it to me," Sharon said. "It's creepy. What does destiny mean anyway?"

"It means what you were meant to do in life," Mr. Fuller replied.

"Do you have a choice about what your destiny is?" Sharon asked.

Her parents looked at one another. "I think each person creates his or her own destiny," Mr. Fuller said.

"But sometimes people have certain talents that they develop in order to be happy," added her mother. "When people talk about destiny they sometimes mean finding out what you were meant to do in life. Why do you ask?"

"No reason," said Sharon, shrugging. She decided not to tell them Miss Lavinia had said music was her destiny. She didn't want to give them any ideas about increasing her music lessons.

The next day, Sharon invited Lori and Sasha to come back to her house after school. "Mom, I'm home," she called as they came through the front door.

"In the living room, dear," called her mother.

Sharon walked to the living room doorway. When she got there, her jaw dropped. Eight women sat in a circle with Mrs. Fuller in the center. All of the women had purple faces!

"Why do they look like that?" Lori whispered to Sharon.

"We're having a Lavender Lady makeup

party," said Mrs. Fuller excitedly. She was the only woman who didn't have purple cream smeared all over her face. "Would you girls like to join us? You're just in time for the facial demonstration."

"No thanks," said Sharon quickly. "We're going upstairs."

"This cream is giving me a rash!" one of the women said suddenly, jumping to her feet.

"Why, that's not possible," Mrs. Fuller said. "Lavender Lady products are very mild and—"

"I *am* getting a rash!" the woman cried. "Look at my arm!"

"Let's get that cream right off you then," said Mrs. Fuller. She tried to wipe the purple stuff off with a tissue, just as the woman turned to reach for her purse. The tissue full of purple face cream fell from Mrs. Fuller's hand and landed on the woman's frilly white blouse.

"My blouse!" the woman cried.

"Oh, dear!" gasped Mrs. Fuller. "I'm so sorry! Sharon, go to the kitchen and get some paper towels."

Sharon did as her mother asked. "Here, Mom," she said, running back into the room to hand her mother the towels.

"If this is going to give me a rash, I want it off right away," said another woman. "I have a PTA meeting tonight. I can't go there covered with a rash."

"Me, too," said yet another woman. "I don't want horrible red bumps all over my skin."

"There's no need to worry," Mrs. Fuller tried to assure the panicky women. "Lavender Lady products have been carefully tested and have been proven to be—"

"Well, I'm not taking any chances," said still another woman, standing up.

Sharon felt so sorry for her mother. This wasn't going well at all. But there was nothing she could do for her. And Lori and Sasha were standing there in the living room, frozen to the spot. They had looks of fascinated horror on their faces.

"Come on," Sharon told them. "Let's go."

She led her friends up the stairs. From the sound of heavy footsteps above them, she suddenly realized her father was home. She was so used to him being at work all the time that she'd forgotten he'd be home.

Oh no, Sharon thought. If Sasha and Lori saw him, they'd know her father wasn't working. "We'll have to be very quiet until we get to my bedroom," she said. "My father's home because he's working on a really big case. He can't be disturbed."

Sasha and Lori nodded and began walking on tiptoe.

But when the girls reached the second floor, they ran into Mr. Fuller. He was wearing a barbecue apron and his arms were loaded with purple boxes. "Hi, hon," he said, when he saw Sharon. "How's it going down there?"

"Not too well," Sharon told him.

Mr. Fuller rolled his eyes. "I can't believe how much of that stuff she ordered. Lavender Lady sent a ton of it over this morning. She'll never sell all this."

"I don't think the face cream will be a big seller," Lori said.

"I don't know where your mother wants me to put all this Lavender Lady junk," Mr. Fuller grumbled as he stumbled up the stairs with the boxes. "I guess I'll just dump it in her study."

Sharon dragged Lori and Sasha down the hall. "That's nice of him to help my mom. Especially since he's so busy," she said as she shut her bedroom door behind her. "Sometimes he takes breaks from his work. It helps him think."

Sasha sat on Sharon's white wicker chair. "My father sometimes stands on his head when he needs to think. He says it gets blood to his brain."

Sharon knew Sasha's father was a writer. At least he *worked* at home. He wasn't carrying purple boxes around.

Lori hopped onto Sharon's bed. "Those ladies sure looked funny, didn't they?" she said, giggling.

"Can you imagine putting that purple goo on your face?" asked Sasha. "Ick!"

"If it makes you more beautiful, why not?" said Sharon.

"My mother wears that stuff," said Lori. "Only hers looks even more disgusting, like she's put cold oatmeal on her face."

"She should call my mother," Sharon suggested. "Purple is better than oatmeal."

"But what if it gives her a rash?" Lori asked.

Sharon just shrugged. "It won't."

They sat and talked about school for a while. "Mr. LaSalle asked me about you the other day, Sharon," Sasha said. "He asked why you weren't trying out for orchestra."

"Orchestra is for geeks," said Sharon.

"Thanks a lot," Sasha said.

"Well, not you. But most of the kids are geeks."

"They are not," said Sasha. "Just because

you like music doesn't make you a geek."

"Rosa Santiago is a geek," Sharon said.

"No, she's not," Sasha disagreed. "She's just smart, and her parents are strict about the way she dresses. Rosa is very nice."

"Whatever," said Sharon. "Well, you guys like music. I don't."

"You don't?" asked Lori. She looked over at the huge pile of CD's stacked next to Sharon's stereo in the corner.

"Of course I like to *listen* to music," said Sharon, rolling her eyes. Sometimes Lori was such a dimwit! "I just don't like playing the flute. My arms get tired, my lips get chapped, and it doesn't look very attractive to be standing there with your cheeks all puffed out like a chipmunk."

"You're not supposed to puff your cheeks," said Sasha.

"Anyway, you should hear Zora Dacyszyn's flute solo. It's awesome." Sasha sat forward excitedly in her chair.

"She's a sixth-grader, isn't she?" Sharon asked. The only thing she knew about Zora Dacyszyn was that she had a heavy accent and a weird name.

"Yeah. And she's really, really good," said Sasha. "Her solo is going to be the best part of the show."

"What show?" Sharon asked.

"There's going to be a big orchestra show before the winter break. Weren't you listening to Mr. LaSalle during music class yesterday?" said Sasha.

Sharon shook her head. "Nope." She'd been too busy worrying about people finding out her father had been fired from his job.

At five o'clock, Sasha and Lori had to leave. Sharon walked them downstairs. Luckily, there was no sign of her father.

Mrs. Fuller sat alone in the living room, her chin in her hands. On the floor around her were little sample packets of Lavender Lady products. She tried to smile when she saw the girls.

"'Bye, Mrs. Fuller," said Lori and Sasha together.

Mrs. Fuller waved to them. Suddenly, she jumped up from her chair. "Lori, Sasha, I want you to give your mothers something from me." She scooped up a handful of sample packets. "Tell them to call me if they'd like more."

Lori turned the packets over in her hands. "Gee, Mrs. Fuller, I don't think my mom wants to get a rash."

Mrs. Fuller sighed. "She won't get a rash. That woman probably ate something she's allergic to this morning. She got all the others upset. They didn't even stay for the free makeup demonstration. But your mother won't get a rash, I promise."

"Okay, Mrs. Fuller," said Lori.

Sharon walked her friends outside to the front stoop. From up on the roof came the sound of a clarinet playing, soft and floating.

"What's that?" asked Lori.

"Oh, nothing," said Sharon. "Nothing at all."

5

"What's the matter?" Sharon asked Sasha in the schoolyard the next day. "You look so sad."

"It's Mr. LaSalle," Sasha said. There were tears in her eyes. "He's in the hospital."

"What!" Sharon cried. "What's the matter with him?"

"He was playing with his band, the one that plays in the park sometimes, and he just fell down." Sasha hid her face in her hands as the tears tumbled down her cheeks.

"Did he fall off the stage?" Sharon asked.

"No, he...just...fainted."

Sharon patted Sasha on the shoulder. "He'll be all right," she said.

Desdemona came up just then. "Is she upset about Mr. LaSalle?"

Sharon nodded. "Do you know what's the matter with him?"

"I heard he's got pneumonia," she replied.

"Gee, and he thought he had a cold," said Sharon.

"Poor Mr. LaSalle," Sasha said, wiping away her tears. "He's so nice. I can't stand to think of him lying sick in a hospital."

"I wonder what will happen with the orchestra show," Desdemona said. Just then, the bell rang for them to line up.

That morning Ms. McCracken taught a science lesson about undersea life. Sharon spent most of it wondering how long it would be before her father found another job—and how soon after that she'd be able to ask for the flowered dress she'd seen in the magazine.

After science, Ms. McCracken went on to history. "Turn to Chapter Ten, please," she told the class.

Sharon skimmed through her thick textbook. In Chapter Nine, the people all looked pretty happy. That was around the 1920s. Sharon liked the straight beaded dresses the women wore then.

But in Chapter Ten everyone looked sad. Chapter Ten was about the 1930s, when so many people became poor.

"Today we'll talk about the Dust Bowl," said Ms. McCracken. "Does anyone know what the Dust Bowl was?"

John Jerome raised his hand and stood. "A big football game in a dirty stadium?"

"Interesting guess, but not correct," said Ms. McCracken. Next she called on Ronnie Smith, who sat slouched in her chair, her long legs sprawled into the aisle. "Ms. Smith, can you tell us what the Dust Bowl was?"

Very slowly, Ronnie got to her feet. "Umm...was it, like, a really gross bowling alley?"

The class laughed. Ronnie glared at them and sat down.

Sharon was about to suggest that the Dust Bowl was a kind of ancient pottery made of dried mud, when Ms. McCracken told them the answer. "The Dust Bowl happened in the Midwest during the Great Depression in the 1930s. There was a great lack of rain called a drought. Crops failed. Farmers lost their farms."

Desdemona raised her hand. "What was the Great Depression?"

"It was a time of worldwide economic trouble," Ms. McCracken explained. "Many, many people lost their jobs and couldn't find new ones."

"No wonder they were depressed," said Desdemona.

Sharon looked down at the picture in her textbook. It was a black-and-white photo of a family. They had a lot of furniture piled into a pickup truck. The parents and a grandmother sat in the front, and two kids were in the pickup. They all looked very tired and sad.

Sharon rubbed her eyes. For a moment she thought she'd seen her own family in that pickup. In the front seat, she'd seen her mother, her father, and herself.

"Ms. Fuller. Ms. FUL-LER!"

Sharon looked up. "Are you all right?" asked Ms. McCracken. "Are your eyes all right?"

Sharon realized she must have been rubbing them very hard. "Oh, sure, Ms. McCracken. I'm all right."

She glanced back down at the picture. Her family was no longer in it. "Something got in my eye, I guess."

Ms. McCracken nodded. Her blue eyes traveled down to the picture. "That's a very sad picture, isn't it?" she said in an unusually soft voice.

"Yes, it is," Sharon agreed.

Ms. McCracken went back to her lesson. Sharon couldn't bear to listen. She couldn't stop imagining her parents and herself trudging out of their brownstone and getting into a battered old pickup. "Where are we going?" she would ask her mother.

"To live with Ronnie Smith and her family," she imagined her mother answering.

The sound of the lunch bell snapped Sharon to attention. The class began to leave for the lunchroom. "May I see you for a moment, Ms. Fuller?" said Ms. McCracken.

Gulping hard, Sharon went to the teacher's desk. "Yes, Ms. McCracken?"

"Have things settled down at home?"

"What do you mean?" Sharon asked.

"The wild celebration," Ms. McCracken reminded her. "Has all the partying died down?"

"Oh, yes," said Sharon, remembering the lie she'd told in class.

"Good," Ms. McCracken said with a sharp nod. "When I saw you rubbing your eyes I thought perhaps you weren't getting enough sleep."

"Oh, no. I'm sleeping fine," Sharon assured her.

Ms. McCracken's eyes seemed to grow bluer as she studied Sharon. "You weren't rubbing away tears, were you?"

"No, no tears," said Sharon.

"Very well," said Ms. McCracken. "Hurry along to lunch then."

Sharon headed toward the door. Then she turned back for the brown bag lunch her father had packed the night before. He'd figured out that they could save almost ten dollars a week if Sharon took her lunch to school instead of buying the hot lunch in the school lunchroom. "Every dollar counts now," he'd said.

Down in the lunchroom, Sharon was the first one at her table. Soon Kathleen Stoppelmeyer and Rosa Santiago joined her. They always brought bagged lunches, too. Next came Annie Tuzmarti. "Sharon, I'm shocked," Annie teased as she took her seat.

"Why?" Sharon asked.

"I've never seen you with a brown-bag lunch." Annie pulled open her own bag. "I used to always get the hot lunch before my mother became so cheap after the divorce."

"My mother says it's more nutritious to bring your own food," added Rosa. "But I wouldn't mind having the hot lunch once in a while."

"Oh, yeah?" asked Desdemona, as she sat down with her hot lunch tray. "Look at this," she said, wrinkling her nose. "Cardboard turkey, barf gravy, and glue stuffing. I bet if you went into the kitchen you really would find huge bottles of glue. I'm sure that's the main ingredient in all the hot lunches."

Normally, Sharon would have agreed. But today the hot lunch smelled especially good. Better than she ever remembered it smelling. She pulled her sandwich out of its plastic bag and slowly peeled it apart to inspect the insides. "How disgusting!" she groaned. "Salami with mayonnaise! My father must have made this sandwich." Was he out of his mind? Who ate salami with mayonnaise?

"I like mayonnaise," Desdemona said. "I like it on everything. I'll trade you."

"Sure," Sharon said happily. But then she wondered why Desdemona was being so generous. Was she feeling sorry for Sharon?

"Forget it," she said, pulling back her sandwich. "I don't need anyone feeling sorry for me. Just because you have money for the hot lunch doesn't mean you're so great."

A shocked look came over Desdemona's face. "Chill," she said. "What's your problem?"

Sharon realized she'd made a big mistake. After all, Desdemona didn't know anything about her father losing his job. No one knew. "Sorry," Sharon said in a small voice. "But I think I'll keep my sandwich."

"Fine," said Desdemona. She sounded annoyed.

No one can ever know about my Dad, Sharon told herself. *Ever.*

With a sigh, she bit into her salami and mayonnaise sandwich.

6

After lunch, the class had English and reading with Ms. Rivers. After a morning with Ms. McCracken, having Ms. Rivers was great. She was so pretty and nice. Sharon loved the way Ms. Rivers wore her hair, in cornrow braids with colorful beads on the ends. Sharon didn't understand why Ms. Rivers had become a teacher when she probably could have been a model.

"Today we're going to try an unusual writing assignment," said Ms. Rivers. "I want you all to take out a piece of blank paper. We're going to write get-well letters to Mr. LaSalle."

"What should we write?" asked Michael Leontes.

"Write what you feel," Ms. Rivers said. "Do you miss Mr. LaSalle? Why? What are the things you miss about him? How does it make you feel having him gone?"

"It makes me feel like life is very unfair," Desdemona spoke up. "Why does someone nice like Mr. LaSalle have to get sick? It would be much better if some mean, kid-hating person would get sick. Someone like…like…"

"MS. McCRACKEN!!!!!!!" the class said, all together.

"Shhhhh, class, please," said Ms. Rivers. She jumped up from behind her desk and hurried to the door. Nervously, she glanced out into the hall. It was as if she wanted to be sure Ms. McCracken wasn't lurking outside the door listening. "It's not nice to wish illness on anyone," Ms. Rivers said as she returned to her desk. "And Ms. McCracken may be strict, but she is *not* a kid hater."

"Want to bet?" muttered John Jerome.

Ms. Rivers shot him a warning look. "But, Desdemona, you make a good point," Ms. Rivers continued. "The world often seems unfair, especially when bad things happen to people we care about. You can write that to Mr. LaSalle."

Some of the kids asked about the orchestra show. What was going to happen to it?

"We're hoping that someone will step in and help," Ms. Rivers told them. She took a stack of papers from her desk. "Please take these home to your parents."

Ms. Rivers handed the notices to Lori Silver, and the kids passed them to one another. Sharon read hers. It said: "The Martin Luther King, Jr., Elementary Orchestra needs your help. Due to the illness of our regular music teacher, we need a parent with extra time and a musical background to help with our first holiday show. Please send a note in with your child if you would be able to help."

Sharon folded the notice and stuck it into her English book. Even though her father was musical, he wouldn't have time. Soon he would find a job. And if he didn't, Sharon didn't want him around school where everyone could see him not working. Besides, she wasn't in the orchestra anyway.

Sharon wrote her letter to Mr. LaSalle.

Dear Mr. LaSalle,
Hi. I hope you feel better. I thought you
just had a cold the other day. You
should have taken better care of your-
self. Everyone really misses you.

Yours truly,
Sharon Fuller

The last class of the day was health, which

Ms. McCracken taught. That meant they all had to go back across the hall to her classroom.

Today Ms. McCracken talked to them about the value of personal cleanliness.

Sharon yawned. What could be more boring? She pulled out a piece of paper and began writing Lori a note.

I bet washing is big news to Ronnie S. Ha! Ha! McCrackpot probably washes her face with scouring pads.

Chuckling to herself, Sharon kept writing. Then she stopped abruptly and put down her pen. A strange feeling had suddenly come over her, as if someone were watching her. Slowly she looked up.

"I'll take that note, Ms. Fuller," Ms. McCracken said.

Sharon's survival instinct took over. She slapped her hand down over the note.

"The note, Ms. Fuller," Ms. McCracken repeated.

Trembling, Sharon handed her teacher the note. Red splotches formed on Ms. McCracken's face as she read it. "I'll see you after class, Ms. Fuller," she said.

"Yes, Ms. McCracken," said Sharon, her voice barely a whisper. For the rest of health class, she sat stiffly straight with her hands tightly clasped. She wasn't listening to the lecture, though. She was too busy worrying. What would Ms. McCracken do to her after class?

When the bell rang, Sharon's heart began to pound. After all the other kids had left, she got up and went to the teacher's desk.

"It is not so much what your note said that disturbs me," Ms. McCracken began. "Believe me, in over thirty years of teaching, I've read much worse. What concerns me most is your lack of attention in class. I'd like you to write an essay on the value of paying attention."

Ms. McCracken took a sheet of paper from her desk. Then she took out a stamp and a red ink pad. With a firm thump, she stamped the paper. "Do your essay on this paper," she said, handing it to Sharon.

Sharon looked at the top of the page. The stamped message said: "This is a punishment assignment. Parent, please sign here."

Oh, no, Sharon thought. "I can't show my parents this," she said aloud.

"And why not?" Ms. McCracken asked.

"Because of everything that's been happening!" she blurted out before she could stop herself.

"What's been happening?" Ms. McCracken asked.

"Umm...nothing," Sharon stammered. "You know, my father's promotion."

Ms. McCracken's eyes narrowed. "Isn't that *good* news?"

"Oh, sure. But everything is so crazy around my house now. My father's working *all* the time. You can practically see steam coming out of his study. And my mother is so busy rubbing his shoulders and bringing him food and helping him so he can work. They really have their hands full. So if I brought something like this home they might lose their minds. Then my mother wouldn't be able to keep things going, and Daddy couldn't work, and everything might fall apart, and it would be all my fault and—"

"Ms. Fuller," Ms. McCracken cut her off. "I get the idea. I certainly wouldn't want you to cause the downfall of your family structure."

"No, that would be awful," Sharon agreed.

"I'm prepared to offer you a choice," Ms. McCracken continued.

"Oh, I'll do anything," Sharon said quickly.

"If you stay after school this Thursday and try out for the orchestra, we will forget about the punishment assignment. The regular tryouts have already been held, but perhaps you can be squeezed in."

Sharon stood stunned. Leave it to Ms. McCracken to pull such a dirty trick! But what other choice did she have? "All right," she agreed miserably.

"Miss Lavinia is a good friend of mine. She told me you have musical talent," the teacher went on.

Sharon couldn't picture stern, unsmiling Ms. McCracken being friends with spacey Miss Lavinia.

"Very well, Ms. Fuller," said Ms. McCracken, getting up from her desk. "I will walk you out of the school." She took her purse from her desk drawer and put on the heavy wool sweater she always had draped on the back of her chair.

Sharon walked out of the classroom with Ms. McCracken. Even though the teacher walked quickly, the halls had never seemed so unending. Finally, they came out to the schoolyard. "See you tomorrow, Ms. Fuller," Ms. McCracken said.

Sharon was relieved to get away from Ms. McCracken. She said good-bye and hurried straight home.

"Anybody home?" she called as she pushed

open the front door and peered inside.

"In here," her father called from the kitchen.

When Sharon walked in, she found her parents sitting at the kitchen table. Her father had a pencil in his hands and a piece of paper in front of him. Her mother's chin was propped thoughtfully on her hands.

"What's up?" Sharon asked.

"I'm glad you're here, honey," her father replied. "We're having a budget meeting."

"A what?" Sharon asked.

"We're planning how to spend our money," Mrs. Fuller explained. "We need to cut some corners until Daddy finds a job and my Lavender Lady sales pick up."

"What kind of corners?" Sharon asked suspiciously.

"Like your allowance, for one thing," said her father.

"What?" Sharon cried. "But I need it!"

"For what?" her father asked.

"For...for...stuff. You know, like bracelets and barrettes, and pizza and stuff."

"I think you have enough *stuff* to last for a while," said Mr. Fuller. "And you'll survive without pizza."

Sharon slumped into a chair. "This is a disaster!"

"We're also cutting out your flute lessons," Mrs. Fuller added.

Sharon perked up at that news. "Really?" She couldn't help smiling. "Oh, that's all right."

Mr. Fuller frowned. "I didn't think you'd be too upset."

"Oh, it's a big disappointment," Sharon said unconvincingly.

"I'm sure," her mother said, fighting back a small smile.

"Don't you think this is too much for me to take all at once?" Sharon said. "Maybe a little allowance would make me feel better."

"Nice try," muttered Mr. Fuller.

Sharon let her shoulders drop. "Being poor is such a nightmare," she said.

"Stop acting so spoiled, Sharon," Mrs. Fuller said firmly. "We're *not* poor. We're just spending less."

"What's the difference?" Sharon asked, throwing up her hands. She flounced out of the room, just as the doorbell rang.

Sharon ran and peeked out the hall window. Annie, Kareem, John, and Kathleen were standing on her stoop. Sharon opened the door.

"Hi," Annie said. "We're going to Luigi's for pizza. Want to come?"

"Sure," said Sharon. "Just let me go ask for my allow…" Today was allowance day. But she'd just been told that no allowance would be coming.

She couldn't tell her friends she had no money. They'd know something was wrong. Maybe they were expecting her to treat, as she often did. Maybe that was even why they'd invited her.

"I don't think I'll be able to go after all," Sharon said. "I just remembered that Mom wants to take me clothes shopping."

"Are you getting that cool dress you wanted?" Annie asked.

"I think so," Sharon lied.

"What happened with McCracken?" asked John.

Sharon confided, "I have to try out for orchestra."

Kareem snorted with laughter.

"Just like Ronnie Smith."

Sharon didn't like the sound of that.

"Did Ronnie make it into the orchestra?" Kathleen asked.

Annie nodded. "Can you believe it? Mr. LaSalle has Lucy Encinas working with her."

"Poor Lucy," said John. Lucy was the newest girl in their class. She'd just moved to Parkside from Arizona. She could play the drums like anything.

"I'd better go," said Sharon, beginning to shut the door. "See you tomorrow."

"You're sure you don't want to come?" Annie pressed.

"Yes, I'm sure. 'Bye." Sharon leaned against the back of the door. That was a close one. She'd almost slipped and gone with them, forgetting she had no money. Then her friends would all have found out that Mr. Fuller had lost his job.

How had everything gone so wrong?

That night, Sharon took her flute from its case on her nightstand. She turned it over in her hands. How could such a plain, round tube of metal be causing her so many problems? She didn't want to be in the school orchestra. But Ms. McCracken was forcing her into it. She was sure to pass her audition. Then she'd be stuck playing the flute after school twice a week.

Sharon put her instrument to her lips and played a piece Miss Lavinia had taught her. Toward the end, she noticed her mother standing in her bedroom doorway. Sharon quickly put the flute down.

"Don't stop," Mrs. Fuller said, coming into the room. "That was lovely."

"No, it wasn't," Sharon said.

"Are you sad about not taking flute anymore?" Mrs. Fuller asked.

"No way!" Sharon said. Then she remembered that she'd pretended to be sad about it. "I mean I'm not *really* sad, no."

"That's what I thought," said her mother.

"I just picked up my flute and started playing. I don't even know why," Sharon admitted.

"You're very good," her mother said. "I didn't realize you'd made so much progress. Has your father heard you play lately?"

Sharon shook her head. "No."

"Why don't you play for him then?" Mrs. Fuller suggested. "Maybe it will cheer him up."

"It might make him feel worse," Sharon pointed out. "You know, since he had to cut out my lessons."

"I guess you're right," Mrs. Fuller agreed.

Just then, the sound of a clarinet came floating down the stairs. "He's on the roof again," Sharon said.

Mrs. Fuller nodded. "Come on upstairs, Sharon. I need you to help me put stamps on some envelopes."

"Are you sending Christmas cards already?" Sharon asked.

"No," her mother replied. "I'm mailing sales letters to every female in the neighborhood, inviting them to come in for a free facial." Sharon had to admire her mother's determination. After the last Lavender Lady disaster, she had expected her to give up.

Sharon followed her mother out into the hall. "What if every female in the neighborhood winds up with a rash?" she teased. "Wouldn't that be funny! It'd be on the TV. A mysterious rash of rashes has swept Parkside due to Claudia Fuller's—"

Her mother hit her playfully on the arm. "Lavender Lady products do *not* cause rashes!"

Sharon was surprised to see that her mother's study was now a real office. All the romance novels had disappeared from the shelves. In their place were cardboard boxes full of Lavender Lady supplies. Mrs. Fuller's desk was no longer a clutter of magazines and greeting cards. It now held an open appointment book, a lavender-colored pencil holder, and a thick lavender book entitled *The Lavender Lady Guide to Great Sales.*

While her mother addressed her sales letters, Sharon licked the stamps and put them on. It didn't take long for her tongue to feel gluey. The job was boring, but it gave her time to think up a great plan.

Tomorrow she would go down to her orchestra audition, try out, and be terrible!

It would be so simple and easy. Why hadn't she thought of it right away?

"A big smile just came over your face," Mrs. Fuller said. "What are you thinking about?"

"Oh, nothing," Sharon replied. "I was just thinking about something funny that happened in school."

"What?" her mother asked.

"It was dumb," Sharon put her off. Actually, the funny thing was the way in which she'd managed to outwit McCracken. First, she'd gotten out of doing a punishment assignment, and now she'd just figured a way out of being in the orchestra.

"By the way, I'll be late coming home tomorrow. So don't worry about me," Sharon told her mother.

"Why will you be late?"

"I'm trying out for the school orchestra," Sharon said.

"Good for you, honey," said her mother, with a big smile. "That way you can keep playing even though you won't have lessons anymore. What good thinking! See? You do like playing the flute."

Sharon carefully licked a stamp. This was working out perfectly. When her parents found out she hadn't passed the tryout, they'd

67

realize it was hopeless and forget this music stuff once and for all.

The next day, Sharon went to school with a spring in her step. She was feeling good for the first time since her father lost his job.

Sitting in Ms. McCracken's class, she wondered which parent had taken over for Mr. LaSalle. At lunchtime she went down the lunchroom stairs behind Lucy Encinas. "Who's leading the orchestra now?" Sharon asked her.

"I don't know," Lucy replied. She tossed her long, silky black hair over her shoulders. "We haven't had orchestra since those notices went home."

Sharon stepped down beside Lucy. "How is it working out with Ronnie on the drums?" she asked in a low voice.

"She's not too bad," Lucy told her, shrugging. "And she's getting better all the time."

"Really?" Sharon said, surprised.

"Really," said Lucy.

Inside the lunchroom, Sharon sat down with Annie and Rosa. "Let's see what gross thing I have for lunch today," said Sharon, opening up her lunch bag. She peeked inside at the sandwich. *"Bologna!"* she cried. "They've got to be kidding! And with mayonnaise again!"

Sharon glanced hopefully at Desdemona, who had come to the table carrying a tray with a plate of ziti on it. "Don't look at me," said Desdemona.

"There are *globs* of mayonnaise on this," Sharon told her.

Desdemona tasted her ziti and made a face. "Don't say I didn't warn you. This ziti tastes like mush with a can of tomato soup dumped over it."

"It's a deal," said Sharon, pushing her sandwich toward Desdemona.

After lunch, Sharon spent the rest of her class time thinking about how she was going to ruin her orchestra tryout. Some of the kids might laugh at her, but it wouldn't matter. At least *she'd* know she was being terrible on purpose.

When the last bell rang, Sharon went down to the auditorium with the other kids. Sasha came up beside her. "I'm so glad you're going to be in orchestra," she said.

"I have to try out first," Sharon reminded her.

"I know. But you'll make it." Sasha slipped her arm through Sharon's and walked into the auditorium with her.

Just then, Ms. McCracken called from the front of the room. "Sharon Fuller! We're so glad to have you join us. We have a few other tryouts today, but why don't you go first?"

Sharon nodded. "What's *she* doing here?" she muttered to Sasha.

"I don't know," said Sasha softly.

Ms. McCracken rapped on the podium with a ruler. "All right, people!" she called. "We're going to begin. I'm taking over for Mr. LaSalle until we find a parent to take his place. So far, no one has come forward. Sharon, why don't you begin your audition?"

Sharon swallowed hard. She'd have to be extra, extra terrible to fool Ms. McCracken. "Play anything you wish, Ms. Fuller," the teacher instructed her.

Sharon took out her flute, being careful to hold it on the wrong side. Then she blew hard, letting out a shrill and deafening sound.

Kids in the front row hunched their shoulders as they covered their ears. Sharon tried hard not to smile. She glanced at Ms. McCracken, but her face showed no expression at all.

Sharon continued to play, fingering the flute with no thought about what she was doing. A few times, she caught herself playing a real piece of music. But she quickly

70

recovered and started blowing all the wrong notes again.

When she'd played for about three minutes, she stopped. The kids around her looked as though they were in pain. Ronnie Smith was laughing. Sasha looked as if she wanted to cry. Rosa just looked confused.

But Ms. McCracken gave Sharon a delighted smile.

"Welcome to the orchestra, Ms. Fuller," she announced.

8

How could this have happened? Sharon wondered as she walked across Harry Park two hours later. Was Ms. McCracken crazy? Surely she didn't think Sharon had played well enough to be in the school orchestra.

With her head down against a cold wind and her fists jammed into the pockets of her jacket, Sharon continued on. Suddenly, a gust of wind blew her studded denim cap off her head. Sharon chased it across the grass. Every time she almost reached it, the cap took off once again.

"Got ya!" Sharon cried finally, stomping on her cap. She realized she had run into one of the playground areas. Lilting notes from a flute made her look over to the right. There was Zora Dacyszyn, the sixth-grade girl who was doing the flute solo in the orchestra show. Sharon had sat behind her in the auditorium. Zora had thick, dark hair and a very round face.

Sharon listened for a few minutes. She was almost as good as the sixth-grader. She could probably even be better, if she practiced. Zora seemed so absorbed in her playing that she didn't even notice her. *What a geek,* Sharon thought.

Sharon continued on home, keeping one hand on her cap so it wouldn't blow away. Ms. McCracken was totally nuts. When the new parent volunteer arrived, he or she would surely see that Sharon didn't belong in the orchestra—not if she kept playing the way she had today. She would just have to keep playing badly until the parent-volunteer arrived. Then the parent would ask her to leave the orchestra and everything would be fine again.

The next day, Sharon couldn't get Zora out of her mind. She wasn't sure why the girl irked her so much.

"I hear you made the orchestra," Annie said to Sharon at lunch. Her brown eyes were shining with laughter. "Rosa told me you were truly awful, too."

"What does Rosa know?" Sharon snapped. Her voice sounded so angry that she surprised even herself.

Annie drew back in her chair. "Sorry," she said. "I thought that maybe you might have...you know...that you played like that on purpose."

Sharon wasn't sure what to say. She didn't want anyone to know that she'd played badly on purpose. They all had to think she was really terrible. That way, when the new parent volunteer came in and asked her to leave, there would be no problem.

"Maybe I didn't have my the best audition, but I made the orchestra, didn't I?" Sharon said sulkily.

"Sure. Yeah, you did," Annie replied.

Rosa arrived at the table just then. She was followed by Sylvie, Desdemona, and Lori. They sat down with their trays. Today Sharon traded her ham and mayonnaise sandwich for Desdemona's pizza. "Why don't you just ask your parents to stop putting mayonnaise on your lunch?" Desdemona asked as she bit into the sandwich.

"Because then you might not trade with me," Sharon confessed.

Desdemona nodded. "That's true," she said.

"Why don't you just buy your own hot lunch?" asked Annie. "Your parents are loaded with money."

"Nutrition," Sharon said, thinking fast. "My parents don't think the hot lunches are good for me."

Desdemona wiped a smear of mayonnaise from her mouth. "They're right. The hot lunches stink. You're lucky to have parents who make you lunch. My mother is so busy she doesn't have time. She hates to cook anyway. Even to make a sandwich."

As Desdemona spoke, Zora Dacyszyn walked by. "Does that girl really bug you?" Sharon asked the others. All of her friends looked at her blankly.

"No," said Lori. "Does she bug *you*?"

"Unbelievably," Sharon said picking up her pizza.

That afternoon, Sharon found herself rushing out of school. At first, she couldn't figure out why. Then she remembered. It was Friday. She had her flute lesson. And if she was late, Miss Lavinia might call her house again.

Sharon practically ran across Harry Park, her flute case banging against her side. She was breathless by the time she got to Elm Street. Panting, she climbed Miss Lavinia's steps.

Then she remembered.

She didn't have flute lessons. Her parents

had already canceled them.

The window nearest the door was open a crack, and music drifted out into the courtyard. Miss Lavinia was playing one of her old-fashioned records.

Sharon wondered how she could have forgotten that her lesson had been canceled. For some reason, she didn't want to leave right away. Maybe she just wanted to hear more of the music. It sounded a little bit sad.

As she stood, listening, Zora Dacyszyn came down Elm Street. She turned right into Miss Lavinia's courtyard. "What are you doing here?" Sharon blurted out.

"I have a lesson today," Zora replied in her thick accent. "A spot opened up at this time, so I grabbed it. Miss Lavinia is the best flute instructor in Parkside. Do you study with her?"

"No. I mean, yes. I mean...I used to," Sharon stammered.

Zora shrugged and rang Miss Lavinia's bell. Sharon didn't want to see her teacher. She didn't want to have to explain what she was doing there. Ducking her head, she hurried away from the house. For half a block, she could still hear the lilting strains of the strange, sad music.

As she came up to her house, Sharon saw

a bunch of women of different ages talking to one another in the small front yard. What was going on?

Slowly, she started down the walk. On her front door she saw a sign printed in purple. It said, "Lavender Lady Open House Here."

How mortifying! Her mother was turning their house into a beauty shop!

Then Sharon spotted Lori Silver's mother. And there was Angelina DuMonde, Desdemona's actress mother. Sasha's mother was there, too. She should have realized this would happen when she was helping her mother send out all those letters. But she'd been too busy worrying about orchestra to think much about it. What if her mother told someone that Sharon's father was out of work?

Turning abruptly, Sharon walked back down the walk. She wanted no part of this!

Without thinking about where she was going, Sharon headed back up Elm Street. She tried not to listen to Zora's playing as she passed Miss Lavinia's. Instead she covered her ears and marched past.

When Sharon reached Grant Avenue, she turned right. Maybe a candy bar from Newton's Newsstand might make her feel better.

She was almost there. Then she remembered. She had no money. None!

Why do I keep forgetting things like this? Sharon thought. *I'm spacier than Miss Lavinia these days.* But her whole life was changing so fast. How could she keep up with all these crazy changes? For the millionth time, she wished her father would find a new job soon. Then everything could get back to normal again.

Just then, she saw Annie, Rosa, Desdemona, and Sylvie coming up Grant Avenue toward her. They were probably heading for Luigi's Pizza Parlor. If they saw her, they'd invite her to come along. She'd have to admit she had no money. They'd know something was wrong.

Sharon didn't want to see her friends. Quickly, she ducked into an alleyway behind Ice Cream Heaven. In the back of the ice cream parlor was a wooden fence with a gate. The gate was open. Sharon could see that it led to another alley, which ran into the string of apartments at the corner of Willow and Grant where Sasha lived.

Sharon darted across the alley so the other girls wouldn't spot her. Then she ran toward the apartments.

Soon she found herself in a quiet little courtyard behind two tall apartment buildings. She decided to turn right and cut back up to Grant Avenue.

Sharon turned and—BAM!—smashed right into someone. The woman's grocery bags flew into the air. A tomato splatted juicily onto the cement. Sharon stumbled backward, and the woman cried out as she tumbled onto a patch of scrubby grass.

"I'm so sorry," Sharon said, rushing to help the woman she'd knocked down.

The woman was still lying on the grass. Slowly she got up onto her elbows. The first thing Sharon saw was a blaze of orange hair.

She'd knocked down Ms. McCracken!

9

"M-Ms. McCracken," Sharon stammered.

Her teacher shook her head slowly from side to side, seeming dazed. Her pile of stiff, red hair was tilted to one side. Then she seemed to snap back to herself. "Ms. Fuller," she said, getting to her feet. "Help me with these groceries."

Sharon scrambled to pick up the food scattered all around them. "I'm so sorry," Sharon said again. "I didn't see you."

"Apparently not," said Ms. McCracken, stooping to pick up a can.

"Do you live in one of these apartments?" Sharon asked, her curiosity getting the best of her. She had never seen Ms. McCracken around this part of town before. In fact, she had no idea where Ms. McCracken lived.

"No, Ms. Fuller," said Ms. McCracken. "I am here to see a friend." She dropped a slightly mashed banana into a brown grocery bag on the ground. Then she pushed her hair back into position on top of her head. Sharon wondered how much hair spray it took to get her hair that stiff.

"Now, Ms. Fuller, you may be of some assistance," said Ms. McCracken. "Pick up one of these grocery bags and follow me."

Excuses leaped into Sharon's mind, but she didn't dare say them out loud. When Ms. McCracken told you to do something, you did it.

Sharon picked up her backpack and a bag of groceries. Then she followed Ms. McCracken into the side door of one of the apartments.

Their footsteps echoed against the hard wooden floor. Sharon stared up at the tall ceilings, which were painted mustard yellow. Very little of the late afternoon light filtered through the frosted glass windows. Sharon thought this was one of the ugliest apartment buildings she'd ever seen. "Where are we going?" she asked Ms. McCracken.

"To see that friend of mine," said Ms McCracken. She began to climb the stairs.

Sharon followed her up three flights. With each flight, the grocery bag she was carrying felt heavier. "Is the elevator broken?" she panted, shifting the bag.

"No," Ms. McCracken replied. "But climbing stairs is excellent exercise. You should always use them."

Sharon blew a strand of hair away from her face. This was more exercise than she'd need for the rest of her life.

On the fifth floor, Ms. McCracken finally turned right. *Thank goodness*, thought Sharon. She followed her teacher to a doorway.

"Put your bag down right there," said Ms. McCracken, pointing to a rough brown doormat. Sharon put the bag down. Then Ms. McCracken handed her one of the two bags she had been carrying. "Come along now."

"Aren't you going to see your friend?" Sharon asked.

"She lives on the seventh floor," Ms. McCracken replied. She was already halfway down the hall. Sharon hurried after her.

"Then who are these groceries for?" Sharon asked.

"Someone who needs them but is too proud to ask for help," said Ms. McCracken, starting back up the stairs. "Everyone needs help at one time or another."

Sharon couldn't imagine Ms. McCracken *ever* needing help.

Finally, they arrived at the seventh floor. At the end of the hall, Ms. McCracken rapped sharply on a door marked 7-G. They waited for several minutes. "I guess your friend isn't home," said Sharon.

Then she heard the clanking sound of locks being opened. "Is that you, Miriam?" came a small, weak voice.

"Yes, it's me."

Sharon's mouth dropped open. Ms. McCracken's first name was *Miriam?*

The last lock clanked open.

"Roll back, Mimi, I'm pushing the door in," said Ms. McCracken. As the door opened, Sharon saw a very old woman in a wheelchair. Sharon had never seen anyone so old. She had white hair, but she was nearly bald. Her face was a mass of wrinkles with two nearly-black eyes shining out. She was wearing a pink bathrobe and had a black-and-white check throw rug over her lap.

"Mimi, this is one of my students, Sharon Fuller. Ms. Fuller, this is my dear friend Mrs. LeDuc."

"It's nice to meet you," Sharon said. She set her grocery bag down on the kitchen counter.

"Likewise," Mrs. LeDuc replied feebly.

From then on, Ms. McCracken was her

bustling, know-it-all self as she moved about the apartment, tidying and dusting. Yet Sharon noticed a difference. Ms. McCracken was a lot nicer with Mrs. LeDuc than she was with her students. She even smiled twice.

Ms. McCracken took a hardcover book from the tall bookshelf in one corner of the room. "Sharon, please read this to Mrs. LeDuc while I fix her some supper," she said. "You don't have to be home right away, do you?"

"Umm, I guess not," Sharon said, taking the book. It turned out to be a cookbook. "These are just recipes," she objected. Maybe Ms. McCracken had given her the wrong book.

"Yes, I know," Ms. McCracken nodded. "She likes to hear them."

"They remind me of when I was a girl," Mrs. LeDuc spoke up.

Sharon opened to the first recipe. "*Lapin á la mou...mou...*I can't say this."

"*Moutarde,*" Ms. McCracken called from the narrow kitchen next door. "That recipe is for rabbit in mustard sauce."

"Oh, yes, that's a good one," said Mrs. LeDuc. "Keep reading, please."

Sharon wrinkled her nose. She couldn't imagine eating a bunny, especially not with mustard. But she read the recipe anyway. "Take one rabbit and brown it in peanut oil." She hoped they took the fur off first. By the time Sharon reached the part where the rabbit was being covered with sauce and laid onto a bed of noodles, Ms. McCracken came into the room with a silver tray.

"Dinner is served," she sang out. She rolled Mrs. LeDuc to a table and laid the dish of macaroni and cheese with ground beef in front of her. Then she went to Mrs. LeDuc's cabinet and took out a record album. Like Miss Lavinia, Mrs. LeDuc didn't seem to have any tapes or CD's. "Shall we have some dinner music?" asked Ms. McCracken.

Soon the room was filled with lovely flute music. The piece was classical and Sharon didn't know it, but the tiny dark apartment seemed changed by it. A dreamy look came over Mrs. LeDuc's face. As if by magic, Sharon could see Mrs. LeDuc as a young woman in Paris, eating rabbit in mustard sauce in a café with a red-checked tablecloth. *Maybe she knows Miss Lavinia,* Sharon thought, remembering the old photo on her flute teacher's mantel.

The image lasted for just a moment. Then Mrs. LeDuc was transformed back into a lonely old woman in a dark apartment eating macaroni and cheese.

After Mrs. LeDuc finished her meal, Ms. McCracken helped her into bed. In minutes, the old woman was asleep. Silently, Sharon helped Ms. McCracken clean up. Then they left the apartment. "The door will lock behind us," she told Sharon.

"Who is that lady?" Sharon asked as they headed back down the hall.

"Mrs. LeDuc was once a neighbor of mine," said Ms. McCracken. "She and her husband owned a restaurant." She locked a steady gaze on Sharon. "You know, Ms. Fuller, helping those who are less fortunate than ourselves can be very rewarding."

Sharon just nodded. She was seeing a whole different side of her teacher this afternoon.

Ms. McCracken went down the stairs. Sharon followed. At the fifth floor, Sharon noticed that the bag of groceries they had left was gone. Ms. McCracken gave a small smile.

"It's really nice of you to help these people," Sharon said sincerely.

"Mrs. LeDuc helped me quite a bit at one time," said Ms. McCracken. "I was trying to complete my college education at night school, and she was very encouraging. I will never forget that. And the woman in 5-C has two children, no husband or family, and isn't getting much help from anyone. Mrs. LeDuc told me about her."

Again Sharon didn't answer. She was beginning to understand that her own family wasn't as badly off as she had thought. At least they had each other.

"You know, Ms. Fuller," her teacher went on, "Ms. Tillman has a long list of volunteer activities you could become involved in. Perhaps you might make an appointment to talk to her about it."

"But community service is just if you get detention," Sharon reminded her.

Ms. McCracken smiled. "I could send you to detention."

"No, thanks," Sharon said quickly. Her teacher was beginning to sound more like her old self.

Once they were outside again, Sharon said good-bye to Ms. McCracken and hurried back up toward Grant Avenue. She was just turning the corner onto Elm when she spotted her father huffing and puffing up the street. "Where have you been?" he cried from half a block away.

Sharon ran to meet him. "Sorry, Daddy. I forgot I didn't have a flute lesson today. I went to Miss Lavinia's by mistake, and then I ran into Ms. McCracken. She wanted me to help her with some stuff. I couldn't say no."

"I was worried sick," her father scolded. "I was just heading up to the park to look for you."

"Sorry, Daddy," Sharon said again. Her father looked really upset. "Is Mom worried?" she asked.

"Your mother doesn't know you're not home yet."

"She doesn't?" Sharon said, surprised.

"No. She's very busy with her open house."

"Oh," said Sharon. She wasn't sure she liked the idea that her mother wasn't concerned about where she was. Sharon and her father walked home together without talking. From his cloudy expression, Sharon could tell her father was still angry.

When they reached their house, the last woman was leaving. Mrs. Fuller waved to her from the doorway. "Remember," she called, "when that scrubbing lotion runs out, I have more. You have my number. Call me."

"I certainly will," the woman called back happily.

Suddenly, Mrs. Fuller noticed Sharon and her father. "Hi, you two," she said brightly. "Have you been in the park?"

"No. Sharon was off having some grand

adventure with Ms. McCracken!" Mr. Fuller snapped as he climbed the steps.

"Well, don't yell at me," Mrs. Fuller shot back. "Sharon was your responsibility today."

"How will I ever find a job if I have to do all the household chores?" Mr. Fuller said angrily.

I'm a household chore? Sharon thought.

Mrs. Fuller followed Mr. Fuller into the house. "How am I going to build this business if I can't rely on you to keep track of our child?"

The door closed and Sharon sat down on the stoop. She slid her backpack off her shoulders and watched as it tumbled down the steps. Her English book and a folder fell onto the path. Sharon didn't feel like picking them up just then. Instead, she sat with her chin on her hands, thinking about everything that had happened that afternoon.

In a few minutes, her father came out and sat beside her. He didn't look happy. "What's the matter?" Sharon asked.

"Oh, nothing," he grumbled.

"How did the Lavender Lady party go?" Sharon asked.

"Great," said her father. "Your mother sold half of the products she bought."

"Hey, that's great," said Sharon.

"Yes, it certainly is," said Mr. Fuller. "Though I must say I'm surprised." Just then, he noticed Sharon's spilled backpack. He slid down off the steps to pick it up. "Don't treat your school things like this, Sharon."

As he was picking up her English book, a paper fluttered to the ground. He picked it up and read it. It was the notice asking a parent to volunteer to lead the orchestra.

Sharon didn't like the interested expression in his eyes. "Oh, that's just nothing, Daddy," she said quickly. "Forget about it."

"I could do this," he said.

"You don't have to. Someone else will do it."

"I didn't even know your school *had* an orchestra." That was because Sharon had never told him. She was sure he'd make her join.

"Well, they do," she admitted.

"Why don't you try out for it?" Mr. Fuller asked, excitement filling his voice.

"Well...umm..." She didn't want to tell him she was already in it since she was hoping to be thrown out.

"I'm going to volunteer," Mr. Fuller said firmly. "As long as I'm not working, I might as well be useful."

"No!" Sharon cried. "You shouldn't feel bad

about being useless. I don't mind. It's fine. Really!"

Mr. Fuller frowned at her. "Thank you, Sharon," he said. "But my mind is made up. Maybe I can even get *you* into the orchestra."

"I'm already in," Sharon said glumly.

"You are?" Mr. Fuller cried, delighted. "And I didn't even know. I've been so concerned about getting a job that I haven't been paying enough attention lately. But all that is going to change."

"Great," said Sharon miserably. "Just great."

Sharon listened outside the kitchen door early Monday morning. Her father was talking on the phone. "Yes, Ms. Tillman, I'd be delighted to take over the orchestra," he said. "You don't have to thank me."

Sharon slumped against the wall. This was another disaster.

"Don't slouch," her mother said as she went past. In her arms were rolls of lavender crepe paper.

"What are you doing with all that stuff?" Sharon asked.

"I'm going to decorate the living room," her mother replied. "The Lavender Lady sales force is having their monthly sales meeting here."

Sharon followed her into the living room. "What do they do at the meetings?"

Mrs. Fuller pulled up a chair and began tying the crepe paper to the chandelier. "Oh, the Lavender Lady director gives us sales tips and there are prizes for the top sellers. We even sing songs."

"What kind of songs?" Sharon asked.

Her mother stopped tying and started to sing. "Lavender Ladies, we sell, sell, sell. Lavender Lady rings the bell, bell, bell. Bing, bong, bing, Lavender Lady's the thing. Bing, bang, bong, this is our selling song. This month nothing can go wrong. I'll be queen of sales! Yeah!" Mrs. Fuller punched her fist into the air.

"That is totally stupid," said Sharon.

"This year Lavender Lady is one of the top ten fastest-growing companies," Mrs. Fuller told her. "People are dying to buy Lavender Lady stock."

Sharon had never seen her mother so enthused about anything—not even last year when her father gave her a new car for her birthday.

Her father appeared in the doorway. "You're looking at the new head of the MLK, Jr., orchestra," he announced.

Mrs. Fuller clapped her hands together in delight. "Why, that's wonderful, dear."

Sharon shook her head in bewilderment. Her parents had both flipped their lids—completely. Her mother was stringing crepe paper all over the house, and her father was going to play orchestra conductor with a bunch of kids.

"You'd better eat something before school," Mr. Fuller said to Sharon. "I got Rice Crackos on sale yesterday. Half price!"

They were definitely cracking up.

Sharon ate her cereal and pulled on her denim jacket. "Have a good day," her father said. "I'll see you after school."

"Today?" Sharon asked.

"Yes. It *is* orchestra day, isn't it?"

"Right," Sharon said miserably. "Mondays and Thursdays."

She had spent all weekend hoping that her father would change his mind. Every time the phone rang, she prayed it was some company offering him a job. But most of the time it was a woman ordering some Lavender Lady product. She'd barely seen her mother all weekend. Mrs. Fuller had spent most of the time upstairs in her office, filling out sales slips and reordering.

There were so many horrible things about her father taking over the orchestra. Number one, everyone would wonder why Mr. Fuller wasn't working. Number two, she'd never get thrown out of the orchestra now!

But what if she was really, *really* terrible? Her father couldn't keep her just because she was his daughter. Or could he?

A cold blast of air sent a chill through Sharon as she opened the front door. She went back to the closet to get out her fake fur leopard-print jacket. It was one of her favorite things.

There were snow flurries on the way to school. Sharon stopped at Sasha's house, but Mrs. Sommers said she'd already left. That was strange, Sharon thought. Sasha usually waited for her. And she wasn't even late today.

In the schoolyard, Sharon met up with Lori. "Did you run away from a bunch of our friends on Friday?" Lori asked.

"Of course not," Sharon lied.

"Sylvie said she and Annie and Rosa and Desdemona saw you run away from them," Lori insisted. "And how come you don't want to go to Luigi's anymore? Is something wrong, Sharon?"

"Why would something be wrong?" Sharon asked.

"Well, I've just had this feeling for a few days now," said Lori. "Over the weekend I decided to ask you, even if you did get mad at me."

"I'm not mad at you," Sharon muttered.

Just then, the lilting notes of a flute made Sharon turn. It was Zora again. Beside her, playing a small round drum, was Lucy Encinas. And Sasha was starting to play her violin.

"Orchestra dweebs," Sharon grumbled.

"Aren't you in the orchestra now?" Lori asked.

"Not because I want to be," Sharon told her.

As Sharon listened to Lucy, Sasha, and Zora play, she thought of how Miss Lavinia wanted a cedar flute. She decided to ask Lucy if she knew where she could get one for Miss Lavinia.

When the piece came to an end, Zora stood up and played "Clair de Lune" by herself.

Even I could play *that,* Sharon told herself.

Some kids clapped for Zora when she was done. Zora nodded at them with that same smug little smile that Sharon was growing to hate more and more.

I'm better than she is, Sharon thought. *Way better.*

But, Sharon reminded herself, she hated the flute, right? So what did she care if Zora got all the attention?

Sharon went over to Sasha. "Why didn't you wait for me this morning?" she asked.

"I wanted to get here early to play with Zora," Sasha said. "We made plans during orchestra on Thursday."

"Why didn't you tell me?" Sharon demanded.

Sasha shrugged. "You left so fast after orchestra on Thursday that I didn't have a chance."

"Well, I was upset about having to be there."

"You haven't been hanging around much with anyone anymore," Sasha pointed out. "You even ran away from us the other day."

"I did not!" Sharon said hotly.

"Annie saw you," Sasha replied. "So did Sylvie."

Sharon folded her arms angrily. "It was someone else."

Finally, the bell rang and everyone lined up for class. Sharon was fuming. Now Zora was taking her lesson time with Miss Lavinia *and* her friends. Sharon didn't like it at all. Not one bit.

During class, Sharon tried hard to pay attention. It wasn't easy, though. For some reason, Ms. McCracken looked different today. Her face seemed a little softer. Her hair didn't seem so bright. Her voice wasn't as harsh. Had McCracken changed? Or had Sharon changed? Sharon wasn't sure.

The other reason she couldn't pay attention was because she was too busy dreading orchestra.

At lunch Annie, Sylvie, and Rosa were cool to her, but Desdemona still traded lunches. After lunch, Ms. Rivers read the class a letter from Mr. LaSalle.

Dear Class,
Thanks so much for your letters. They really brightened my day. I am out of the hospital now and feeling much better. My doctor wants me to rest for a while longer, but I am trying to talk him out of it. Keep those cards and letters coming. I miss you all.
Sincerely,
Ed LaSalle

Sharon hoped Mr. LaSalle was a good talker. The sooner he was able to talk his doctor into letting him return to work, the sooner he'd throw her out of orchestra.

Usually Sharon counted the minutes until the final bell rang. Today she wished school would go on forever. But three o'clock came as always. It was time for orchestra.

Sharon slowly got her things and headed down to the auditorium. As soon as she came through the door, Rosa put her hand on her arm. "Why is your father here?" Rosa asked.

Sharon sighed. "You'll see."

When everyone was seated, Mr. Fuller stepped onto the stage. "Hi, everyone. I'm Alex Fuller. I'll be taking over as orchestra leader while Mr. LaSalle's gone. I spoke to him today on the phone. He says to tell you all that he expects a great show. He's going to be there in the audience. So let's do our best and make him proud."

Sharon's father looked around at all the faces. "I'm making one change right away. We're moving from here to the gym. I know Mr. LaSalle wanted you to get used to the sound in here, but I want you to forget about all that. I want you to spread out and fill that gym. We are going to cut loose and really get down."

Sharon covered her face with her hands as she slumped into her seat. *Cut loose? Get down?* Where was her father getting these expressions?

Everyone got up and moved to the gym. Mr. Fuller arranged to have the big instruments moved in there, too. "Today I'm going to teach you something new," Mr. Fuller said when they were all settled. "It's a song called 'Good Lovin'.' Do any of you know it?"

Sasha raised her hand. "My mother plays it real loud and dances all over the apartment while she cleans."

Sharon shot Sasha a shocked look. She couldn't picture Mrs. Sommers doing that.

Mr. Fuller laughed. "That's the one." He handed them photocopied sheets of music with the words and notes of the song on them. Then he organized the orchestra into the different families of instruments. "There's a great drum part in this," he told Lucy and Ronnie as he helped them tighten up loose parts on their drums. "We'll have to work on who plays what part."

Sharon was beginning to see a whole new side of her father. She had never known him like this—so filled with enthusiasm. The kids seemed to like him, too. They were all smiling and excited.

It took most of the hour to slowly go over the song and figure out the different parts. "Let's try it all the way through, just for fun," Mr. Fuller said when it was almost time to leave.

Everyone tried to play. They were all pretty awful since no one really knew the parts yet. Mr. Fuller raised his hand and stopped the music. "Does someone over here have a broken instrument?" he asked, walking over to the woodwind section.

All of the kids turned and looked at Sharon. "I guess it's me, Daddy," she said.

"Is something wrong with your flute?" Mr. Fuller asked, frowning.

"I don't think so," she said.

"Play it again."

Sharon knew this was her big chance. But it was hard to play badly in front of her father. All her life she'd tried to make him proud. Now she'd have to do just the opposite.

Sharon put her lips to her flute and blew. She fingered senselessly just as she'd done during tryouts.

Mr. Fuller's jaw dropped. "Thank you, Sharon," he cut her off. "That's enough. I think your flute *is* broken."

"She could try mine," Rosa offered, wiping the mouthpiece with a tissue.

Mr. Fuller took the flute from Rosa and handed it to Sharon. "Try this one."

Sharon again played with ear-splitting notes.

"I guess it's not the flute," said Mr. Fuller.

Over her father's shoulder, Sharon saw Zora snickering. Someone behind Zora giggled. Then someone else laughed, too. "Sorry, Daddy," Sharon murmured.

"Okay, everyone," Mr. Fuller said to the orchestra. "See you all on Thursday. Remember to practice."

The kids packed their instruments and began leaving the gym. No one asked Sharon anything about her dad. But she didn't feel happy. She felt terrible. Today had gone even worse than she'd expected.

On the way home from school, Sharon and her father passed Miss Lavinia's house. Sharon noticed that her old teacher had already put up a Christmas wreath. She was glad it was cold so they wouldn't hear the flute music wafting out the window.

"Daddy, did I embarrass you today?" Sharon asked finally.

"No, sweetie, not embarrassed. Not exactly. I mean, Mr. LaSalle thought you were good enough to make the orchestra, so..."

"Mr. LaSalle didn't pick me," Sharon corrected him. "Ms. McCracken let me in."

"Ms. McCracken?" Mr. Fuller asked, surprised. "Is she a musician?"

"No. She was just filling in."

"I suppose that explains it," said Mr. Fuller.

"Explains what?" Sharon asked. She knew full well what he meant, but she just wanted to hear him say it. He really thought she was a terrible flute player.

"Oh, nothing," Mr. Fuller said. "Everyone is entitled to an off day. I'd say your playing was a little off today."

"Face it, Daddy!" Sharon wailed. "I'm the worst!"

"No, no, I wouldn't say that. It's just that all this time I assumed you took after me. You know, that you had my love for music. But maybe you take after your mother and her side of the family."

"Doesn't Mom like music?" Sharon asked.

"Sure, she likes it, but she's not very musical herself."

That didn't sound so bad. But the disappointment in her father's eyes was hard to take. He had thought they were alike. Now he knew they weren't. To her surprise, Sharon wanted to shout, "We *are* alike. I *am* like you!" But she couldn't.

This was going all wrong.

"Maybe Miss Lavinia wasn't the teacher I thought she was," Mr. Fuller said sadly.

"Oh, no! She's a great teacher!" Sharon said, surprised at her own forcefulness. "The way I play isn't Miss Lavinia's fault."

Mr. Fuller shook his head. "Then whose fault *is* it?"

Mine! Sharon wanted to shout. Why couldn't she just tell her father the truth? *She hated flute!*

But did she really?

Sharon and her father walked the rest of the way to their house in silence. When they arrived, the living room was full of women. One woman in a lavender suit was standing at an easel, pointing to a graph with a wooden pointer.

"As we come into the holiday season, you can expect a dramatic jump in sales," she said. "But be prepared for a drastic slump as people start paying their holiday bills." As she spoke, she followed the graph line downward.

Mrs. Fuller waved and smiled when she spotted her husband and Sharon.

"I'm going to start dinner," Mr. Fuller said to Sharon in a low voice.

"I'll come help you in a minute," Sharon told him. She needed some time alone first.

Sharon went upstairs and took her flute from its case. She played "Clair de Lune" as well as she could. As she played, she thought of Miss Lavinia telling her that music was her destiny. Could she possibly be right?

Then Sharon thought about Lucy Encinas. Lucy always seemed so happy when she played. Suddenly Sharon was overwhelmed with the desire to forget about everything— her father's job, the dress she wasn't getting, whether or not she wanted to be in the orchestra—and just lose herself in the music.

As Sharon hit a high note, Lucy melted from her mind, and Zora's face appeared. Suddenly Sharon realized why Zora bothered her so much. Zora wasn't afraid to be good at something. She didn't care what anyone thought of her. Sharon was jealous of that.

Sharon stopped playing and put down her flute. She didn't hate Zora after all. She hated the fact that Zora had something she wanted. Zora wasn't afraid to let the music inside of her out.

Sharon bolted out of her room and rushed down the stairs. The women in the living room were singing their Lavender Lady song: "Bing, bang, bong..."

Sharon ran into the kitchen. "Dad!" she said.

"Just a minute, hon," her father said, holding up one hand. He was on the kitchen phone. "I'm very sorry to hear that. How awful. Well, I hope she feels better. 'Bye."

"What's wrong?" Sharon asked.

"That was Mr. LaSalle. He called to tell me that Zora Dacyszyn fell off her bike over the weekend. She broke her arm."

"That's too bad," said Sharon. She felt truly sorry for Zora.

"Poor kid," said Mr. Fuller. "She was going to do a solo performance of 'Greensleeves' for the show."

"I can do it," Sharon said, almost without thinking.

"Sharon...I don't know..."

"I *can*, Daddy," said Sharon. She raced back upstairs, grabbed her flute, and raced down again. She took a deep breath in the kitchen doorway. "Listen."

Sharon played "Greensleeves" with all the skill she possessed. The concerned line on her father's brow slowly uncreased. He looked really surprised. Then his eyes slowly grew wider and a smile formed on his lips.

When Sharon finished playing, she was startled by the sound of clapping behind her. She turned and saw that the Lavender Lady saleswomen had gathered in the hallway to listen. "Lovely, just lovely," said the woman in the lavender suit.

Sharon just smiled brightly.

That night as Sharon was getting ready for bed, her mother came in. "I was so proud of you today," she said, sitting on Sharon's bed. "You played so beautifully. All the saleswomen were impressed."

"Thanks," said Sharon as she crawled under the covers. Her fashion magazine tumbled from the bed onto the floor.

Mrs. Fuller picked up the magazine and opened to the page Sharon had folded down. It was the picture of the blue flower-print dress.

"This dress would look beautiful on you," Sharon's mother said.

"I thought so, too," Sharon said. "But we don't have the money for it."

Her mother smiled. "I just got my first check from Lavender Lady today," she said.

"Was it enough to buy the dress?" Sharon asked.

Her mother nodded, a happy twinkle in her eye. "I think so. Why don't we go shopping soon?"

"Well, thanks, Mom," Sharon said. "But I have another idea, if that's okay."

Sharon smoothed down the bow at the hip of her red velvet dress. She hoped no one would remember the dress from last year. With the ruffled petticoat slip under it, it looked a little different and still fit. The blue flower-print dress would have looked nicer. But Sharon didn't mind that much.

She peeked out from behind the thick stage curtain. Soon it would be drawn to the side and the orchestra show would begin.

The parents began taking their seats. Her mother was coming down the aisle. Several women waved to her. Since Mrs. Fuller had become the local Lavender Lady saleswoman, it seemed everyone knew her.

Lucy Encinas came up beside Sharon and tapped her shoulder. "I have that cedar flute you asked me about."

"Great! Thanks. Where did you get it?"

Sharon asked. Last week she'd asked Lucy where she could get a flute for Miss Lavinia, but Lucy wasn't sure.

Lucy handed Sharon a wooden case. "Here," she said. "My aunt is visiting from Arizona. I asked her to bring me one. She's a doctor on a reservation, and she knows a musician there who carves them."

Sharon took the flute. "Can I pay you after the show?"

"Sure," Lucy agreed.

"Okay, musicians," said Mr. Fuller as he hurried about backstage. "This is it. Showtime!"

Sasha came up behind Sharon and Lucy. "Mr. LaSalle is in the audience," she said. Sharon scanned the crowd and spotted him.

"He's thinner," Sharon said.

"At least he's well enough to come to the show," said Sasha.

"Chat later, kids," said Mr. Fuller. "Take your positions."

"Let's go," said Sharon, and the three girls went out onto the stage. Sharon sat on a folding chair in the flute section next to Rosa. All around them were whistles, toots, the twang of strings, and the clash of cymbals. Everyone was getting ready. Lucy and Ronnie Smith took their seats behind the drums. Even Ronnie looked excited.

"Nice dress," said Rosa. "But weren't you getting a different one?"

"I liked this one better," said Sharon. "And I needed the money for something else." So what if people knew she was broke?

"Well, it's very pretty, anyway," said Rosa.

Mr. Fuller rushed onstage, pulling on his blue suit jacket. It seemed a little strange to see him in a suit again. "All right, kids," he said. "We're about to go on. Good luck." He turned and nodded to Annie and John. They were the official curtain pullers.

As the curtain opened, the audience clapped loudly. "Welcome to the first-ever performance of the Martin Luther King, Jr., Elementary Orchestra," Mr. Fuller said. "We'll begin with 'A Whole New World,' from the movie *Aladdin*."

The bright lights made it hard to see into the audience. But as she played, Sharon peered out anyway, trying to find familiar faces. She spotted several parents she knew, and Zora, with her arm in a sling. Ms. McCracken was there, of course. Next to Ms. McCracken, Mrs. LeDuc sat in a wheelchair in the aisle. And on the other side of Ms.

111

McCracken was Miss Lavinia.

Sharon felt very happy to see her old teacher. She wanted Miss Lavinia to be proud of her today.

The show began. At first there were a few sour notes. Jimmy Wong forgot his violin part at the end of "We Are the World." But as everyone relaxed and warmed up, the show got better and better.

When the time came for Sharon's solo, she stepped forward to a music stand in the middle of the stage. The audience was completely silent. Sharon took a deep breath and began to play "Greensleeves." Closing her eyes, she put all her attention into the music.

When she finished playing, the audience clapped loudly. From the look of pride on her father's face, Sharon knew she had done well.

The next song was a jazz piece her father had taught them. It was called "Sing, Sing, Sing." It had a long, wild, drum piece in the middle. Ronnie and Lucy threw themselves into it. At the end, Ronnie even threw her drumstick in the air and hit Jimmy Wong on the head.

The last song was "Good Lovin'," and they played it perfectly.

At the very end, the audience got to their

feet and applauded. Mr. Fuller had all the kids get up and bow. He called Mr. LaSalle up on the stage and said he deserved credit for getting the orchestra started. Mr. LaSalle said Mr. Fuller deserved a hand for keeping things going. The audience clapped loudly for both of them.

Finally, the curtain closed and the orchestra members left their seats. Mr. Fuller gave Sharon a hug. "You were great, sweetie," he said proudly.

Sharon hugged him back. "Thanks, Daddy." Then she noticed that her mother had come backstage.

"Great work, Sharon. Beautiful," her mother said.

"Thanks, Mom," said Sharon. She lowered her voice. "Mom, do you think I could have that money now? To buy the cedar flute I told you about for Miss Lavinia? Lucy found one for me."

Mrs. Fuller nodded. "Of course, honey. I'll write your friend a check right now."

Sharon directed her mother over to Lucy. Then she took the cedar flute from the corner where she'd left it and went out into the audience to find Miss Lavinia.

Sharon met up with her old teacher as soon as she walked down the side steps. "Oh, there you are, Sharon," said Miss Lavina, beaming. "I was so proud of you. So proud. I want you to know that you are the winner of the Miss Lavinia Music Scholarship."

"The what?" Sharon asked, confused.

"You've won a year of free flute lessons."

"I didn't know there was a scholarship," said Sharon.

"You're the very first winner," Miss Lavinia said with a smile. "Will you accept?"

"Yes," said Sharon. "Thank you. I've really missed our lessons."

"I'm glad," said Miss Lavinia. "I wasn't sure you would."

"I got this for you," Sharon said, suddenly feeling a little awkward. She handed the flute to Miss Lavinia.

Miss Lavinia opened the box. "A cedar flute," she murmured. "Wherever did you get this?"

"A friend of mine got it from a Native American flute maker."

"Sharon, this is too generous," said Miss Lavinia. "I know your parents had to cancel your lessons and—"

"It's all right," said Sharon. "Mom has a real good job now, and my dad will find something soon. I wanted you to have this."

Miss Lavinia's eyes searched Sharon's

face. What was she seeing? "Thank you, my dear," she said. She squeezed Sharon's hands in her small bony ones. "Come after school, four o'clock this Monday. We will continue as usual."

With a small wave, Miss Lavinia left. Sharon watched her join Ms. McCracken and Mrs. LeDuc as they left the auditorium.

Mr. and Mrs. Fuller came up behind Sharon. "Did Miss Lavinia like her flute?" Mr. Fuller asked.

"She loved it," said Sharon. She turned to her mom. "I know it cost more than the dress I wanted," she said. "Can I work some of it off by helping with your Lavender Lady stuff?" Sharon asked.

"Good idea," Mrs. Fuller said with a smile. "I just happen to have a stack of new brochures waiting to be stamped."

"So how about going to Chang's to celebrate with a great Chinese dinner?" Mr. Fuller suggested.

"Can we afford it?" Sharon asked.

"On this special occasion, I think we can," he answered.

The three of them got their coats and walked out of the school. Snow flurries were starting to fall from the sky. They hurried along the edge of the park until they reached

Chang's Chinese Restaurant on Grant Avenue.

As Sharon was eating her wonton soup, Mr. Fuller suddenly tapped his water glass with his chopsticks. "Attention, please. I have good news for you both." He looked at his wife and Sharon with excited eyes. "I was offered a job today. Two jobs, in fact."

"That's great!" Sharon cried.

"The jobs we spoke about?" Mrs. Fuller asked.

Mr. Fuller nodded. "That's right."

"What jobs?" Sharon asked.

"Well," Mr. Fuller began. "Your mother and I have been talking about this for a few days. Working for a big law office wasn't making me happy. It was so cold and impersonal. I kept it because it paid a lot of money. But now I've decided to make a career change. I'm going to be a public defender."

"What's that?" Sharon asked.

"It's the lawyer the court appoints to represent people who can't afford their own lawyers," Mr. Fuller explained. "I won't make as much money as before, but I'll really feel like I'm doing something to help people." He reached across the table and took his wife's hand. "I couldn't do this if your mother wasn't working now."

"I don't mind at all," said Mrs. Fuller. "I like selling Lavender Lady."

Sharon was happy for her dad, but she was still curious.

"What's the other job?" she asked.

"I'm going to play the clarinet with Ed LaSalle's band."

"That's not a real job," said Sharon.

"Yes, it is," Mr. Fuller said. "It doesn't pay much, but it pays."

Sharon could see that her parents were thrilled with their new plans. Maybe they wouldn't have as much money as before, but she had a feeling they were all going to be much happier.

The waiter brought their order. He placed the plates of sesame noodles, beef with broccoli, and shrimp in lobster sauce on the table. "Eat up," said Mr. Fuller. "This may be our last dinner out for some time."

Hungrily, Sharon scooped the food onto her plate. The food at Chang's had never seemed so delicious.

13

"I think the Meals-on-Wheels program is the one I want to try," Sharon said.

The principal leaned back in her chair. "I must say, Sharon, this is something of a surprise. What made you decide to volunteer?"

"It was something Ms. McCracken said, about how we all need help once in a while," Sharon said. "Or maybe it was those Dust Bowl people."

Ms. Tillman looked confused. "Who?"

"Just some sad-looking people in my history book," Sharon replied. She didn't want to tell Ms. Tillman that she'd imagined the people in the history book were her own family. The principal would probably think she was crazy.

Ms. Tillman gave her a phone number. "And you might want to talk to Alice O'Neal in Ms. Rivers's class. She volunteers every

Saturday. She started working with Meals-on-Wheels as a detention, but she stayed with it."

"Okay. Thanks, Ms. Tillman." School was over for the day, so Sharon walked out the main door. Ms. McCracken was just going down the cement path. Sharon hung back, so she wouldn't have to walk with her.

But Ms. McCracken stopped at the end of the school walk. Without even turning she said, "Have a nice weekend, Ms. Fuller."

She *does* have eyes in the back of her head! Sharon thought. "Thank you, Ms. McCracken," she said. "You, too."

As Sharon neared her house a few minutes later, she saw her mother hurrying out with her lavender supply case. "Hi, honey," she said when she saw Sharon. "I've got to run. Mother Superior over at St. Andrew's wants me to put together a beauty basket as a prize for their big raffle. It's great advertising. This could open up a whole new market for me."

"Good luck," said Sharon as her mother scurried past her.

Her mother waved. "Dad doesn't have to be in court until six," she called. "I should be back by then."

When Sharon went inside the house, her

father was running down the hall with a mop. "Is she gone?" he asked Sharon.

Sharon nodded. "What's wrong?"

"The pipe from the upstairs bathroom burst," Mr. Fuller explained. "I didn't want your mother to know so she wouldn't be upset before she left for her appointment."

Sharon looked up at the ceiling. "I don't see any water leaking."

Mr. Fuller threw open the front hall closet.

"Oh," said Sharon. Water was pouring down onto all the coats.

Mr. Fuller started loading coats into Sharon's arms. "Here, help me get these out before they're all ruined."

As the two of them piled soggy coats on the stairs, Sharon sniffed the air. "Is something burning?"

"My lasagna!" Mr. Fuller cried, running into the kitchen. At the same moment, the smoke detector began its high-pitched *whoop! whoop!*

"Sharon, fan that thing!" Mr. Fuller cried. "We'll have the fire department here."

Sharon grabbed a scarf off her mother's damp coat. Then she jumped up at the smoke detector in the hall, waving the scarf at it. The smoke detector kept right on whooping.

Just then, the phone rang. Thinking it might be the fire department, Sharon grabbed the living room phone. Her father was already on the kitchen extension. "Yes, we're sorry we're a little late with that payment," he said to someone on the other end. "We'll get it to you right away."

Sharon went back to waving at the smoke detector. Her father finally hit it with his mop, and the whooping stopped.

Mr. Fuller shook his head. "The dinner is ruined, the plumber can't come until tomorrow, and the Jiffy credit card company is canceling our credit cards."

Sharon just nodded. What could she say?

Mr. Fuller went to the kitchen and got a bucket. He placed it under the leak in the closet. Then he went over to the front hall table and reached underneath. He came up with his clarinet and Sharon's flute case.

Sharon followed her father up the stairs. On the way, Mr. Fuller grabbed two of the drier jackets, one for himself and one for Sharon. Then they went all the way to the third floor and out onto the roof.

It was a cool, clear winter afternoon. Sharon's nose and ears tingled in the cold, but it didn't bother her. From the roof, she could see all the way up to the park and down to the river at the end of Parkside. The fading sunlight bounced off the buildings, making them gleam with soft color.

Mr. Fuller began to play, and Sharon joined in. She hadn't felt this happy in a long, long time.

Don't miss the next book in the
McCracken's Class series:
McCracken's Class #7:
SAM THE SPY

Sam crept silently to the door outside her mother's study. Her mom was sitting at her desk, talking on the phone.

"Maybe it's time Sam changed schools," Ms. Tillman was saying. "After all, Martin Luther King, Jr., Elementary is a very good school now. And the Academy gets more expensive every year."

Sam couldn't believe she was hearing this. Her mother couldn't really be *serious*.

"Well," her mother went on, "Ms. Rivers's class is full. I'd have to put Sam in Ms. McCracken's class."

Sam almost had a heart attack. She'd heard kids in the neighborhood talking about Crack-the-Whip McCracken.

"Ms. McCracken may be a bit old-fashioned, but she's a fine teacher," Ms. Tillman continued. "She doesn't let her students get away with anything. In fact, she might be exactly what Samantha needs."

That did it. Sam bolted into her mother's study. "No!" she shouted.

Riding Academy

If you love the kids in McCracken's Class, you'll want to meet the girls at the Riding Academy, too! Join Andie, Jina, Mary Beth, and Lauren as they find fun, friends, and horses at a boarding school with an extra-special riding program.

RIDING ACADEMY, a new series from Bullseye Books